A HAVEN ON THE BAY

A WILLA BAY NOVEL

NICOLE ELLIS

LEAPING RABBIT PRESS

1

Meg

Meg Briggs pried the final pansy from the black plastic tray and shook off the loose dirt before placing it in the hole she'd dug with a garden trowel. She patted it into place and leaned back on her heels to survey her handiwork. Before she'd started planting that day, only tufts of knee-high wild grass had bordered the front of the old barn at the Inn at Willa Bay.

Now, purple, pink, and white flowers brightened the exterior of the structure, contrasting sharply with the peeling white paint. She stood, brushing plant debris off her pants before taking a final look. Someday, the whole place would be revitalized. For now, though, this small patch of color would have to do.

A little time remained before she had to get ready for her dinner with Theo, the man she'd been dating for the last few months, so she walked around to the opposite side of the barn and sat down on a stone bench. Next to her, the bushes rustled as a brisk breeze swept through them. In the distance, an eagle cried out as it swooped down toward the bay to pluck an unlucky salmon from below the surface. She leaned against the barn's siding and drew her knees up to her chest, gazing out at the deep blue waters of Willa Bay, and allowing her thoughts to wander and her body to relax.

At times, it seemed like her life had changed a lot in the last few months, but at other times, it was as though she was an actor in a slow-motion movie. When she'd signed the contract to buy the resort with her friend, Zoe, and Zoe's boyfriend, Shawn, it had been with the understanding that they'd get the Inn and the grounds in working order before doing anything else. Later, they'd renovate the old barn into a restaurant for Meg to manage.

Originally, Meg had been fine with that agreement. There wasn't enough time or money to simultaneously take on all of the necessary projects to turn the resort into an event venue. The restaurant was a lower priority in comparison to everything else on the list. She truly was happy for Zoe to realize her dream of operating the premier wedding venue in the Pacific Northwest, but Meg badly wanted to see her own dreams come to fruition as well. She closed her eyes and inhaled the warm salt air. *All in good time.*

The last time she'd talked to Zoe and Shawn, they'd discussed moving up the barn remodel to sometime in early October and postponing their plans to fix up the twenty guest cottages perched above the beach. But starting earlier came with a catch—Meg had been charged with clearing out half a century's worth of storage from the building by the end of September. If she could complete that task in time, they'd proceed with the renovations. If not, they'd need to do the cottages first.

If everything worked according to plan, her restaurant

could be open as soon as January. The project timeline was ambitious, but Zoe had already worked wonders in getting the Inn ready for their first wedding tomorrow, and Meg didn't doubt her friend could pull it off. January still seemed far away, but three months had flown by since they bought the Inn from Celia in April. Meg could wait another five or six months for her restaurant to be completed.

"Oh, there you are," said a woman's voice behind her. Meg turned to see Zoe standing about five feet away, shading her eyes so she could see Meg against the glare of the sun.

"I was just planting some flowers in front of the barn." Meg grinned. "I was planning on checking in with you before I left, honest."

Zoe's laughter bore a nervous tinge. "I figured you would. I just had a few details to go over before tomorrow. I saw your flowers though. They look nice."

Meg glanced at the iPad Zoe held in her hands and raised an eyebrow. "Only a few things?"

Zoe regarded the iPad ruefully. "Okay, okay. Maybe more than a few. Remember, the wedding is at one o'clock tomorrow afternoon. Shawn will manage the parking, and Tia and I will coordinate the ceremony and reception, but I need you to circulate and make sure nothing goes awry."

"It's going to be great." Meg got up from the stone bench and walked over to Zoe. "You and Tia have been slaving over the schedule for weeks. Nothing is going to go wrong."

"Something always goes wrong." Zoe frowned, her eyes scanning the tablet's screen.

Meg held up her hand. "If it does, we'll figure it out. Between you, me, Tia, Celia, and Shawn, we'll have it covered."

Zoe's shoulders slumped. "I hope you're right."

"I know I'm right." Meg gave her a hug, then glanced at her watch. "I'd better leave now to meet Theo though. I'm supposed to pick him up at the marina in twenty minutes."

Zoe took a deep breath. "Have fun."

Meg patted her arm reassuringly. "I will. Now go take a bubble bath or something. You're a ball of nerves."

Her advice was met with a meek smile. "Maybe I should do that after dinner." Zoe stared at her list again and Meg doubted there was much self-care in her friend's near future.

"You should," Meg said firmly. "I'll see you tomorrow, and I expect to hear all about your relaxing evening." She trotted off toward the Inn, where she'd left a dress to change into before her date. She was looking forward to dinner, as they had reservations for a steakhouse in a nearby city. Her stomach grumbled, reminding her that she'd only had time to scarf down a granola bar for lunch while they'd all worked their way through Zoe's massive to-do list. Maybe she needed to take her own advice about self-care.

Twenty minutes later, Meg walked down the dock to Theo's slip at the marina. The rough wooden slats creaked and bobbed underfoot. Some people might be unnerved by the uneven footing, but she'd grown up in Willa Bay and had been around boats her entire life. She wasn't sure she'd want to live on one like Theo did, but there was definitely something appealing about the freedom of being out on the water.

When she reached Theo's boat, she found him sitting

on the deck at the stern, repacking his tackle box. He wore jeans and a paint-stained t-shirt—not what she'd expect for a night out on the town. He lifted his head when she approached.

"Hey," he said, flashing her a toothy smile. "You look nice."

Her cheeks warmed and she smoothed the knee-length skirt of her dress against her legs. "Thanks." She cocked her head to the side. "Uh, are you planning on changing?"

His eyes flickered down to his shirt and he laughed, jumping to his feet. "Oh, yeah. Give me a minute and I'll swap this out for something nicer."

"No problem." A breeze rippled the surface of the water and chilled Meg's bare arms. She shivered and crossed them over her chest, wishing she'd worn a sweater over her dress. It was cooler on the water than it was back on shore. She couldn't complain too much about the weather though. The thermometer had read eighty-five degrees earlier that day, and some of the warmth still lingered in the air.

Five minutes later, Theo climbed off the boat onto the dock behind her. "Okay, I'm ready. Where did you say we were going tonight?" He'd changed into a pair of charcoal-gray slacks and a pinstriped, button-down shirt in a shade of blue that accentuated his dark eyes. He flashed her a slightly lopsided grin and her heart skipped a beat. She'd always been attracted to slender-built men with blond hair, and Theo was no exception.

She tore her eyes away from his physique and returned his smile. "We have reservations at Finnerton's Grill in Everton. They're known for their seafood dishes, so I thought they'd be good to check out. The restaurant at the Inn at Willa Bay may not open for a while, but I'd like to start building my repertoire of recipes now."

His forehead creased into a shallow frown. "Oh man, I was hoping for a steak tonight." Then he shrugged and his lips turned upward into his customary happy-go-lucky grin. "But seafood sounds good too."

"I think they have steak on the menu." She'd read everything she could find about Finnerton's, hoping to learn how they achieved almost a five-star rating out of hundreds of reviews. Normally, online reviews were written by customers who were either extremely pleased or horribly unhappy with their experience at an establishment. To get close to a five-star average was quite a coup, and she was excited to experience the restaurant for herself.

"Great. Surf and turf it is." They neared the end of the ramp leading from the docks to the parking lot and he reached for her hand, squeezing it lightly. His touch was warm and comforting as his fingers intertwined with hers, although the electric tingles from early in their relationship had faded away after the first few weeks. When they reached her car, he broke away from her and waited next to the passenger side for her to unlock the door.

Theo didn't want to remain tethered to any one spot, so the only vehicle he owned was his boat. While Meg didn't mind always being the driver, it did leave her wondering if he'd ever settle down in one place, or if he intended to always be a wanderer. When she'd lived in Portland, she'd enjoyed her freedom, but had also greatly missed her family. Being constantly on the move like Theo would be fun for a while, but not for the long-term.

The drive to Finnerton's took thirty minutes. By the time they arrived and parked, Theo's light banter had eased some of Meg's troubles. Before they entered the restaurant, she stopped and appraised the exterior, wanting to take in every minute detail.

Finnerton's was located on the river that ran through the center of Everton. The entrance from the parking lot wasn't terribly memorable. A few concrete steps led up to a wide front door, offset from the center of a façade plastered with dark cedar shingles. The name of the restaurant had been hand-lettered on an unassuming sign next to the door. However, the parking lot was almost full —always a good sign in the restaurant business.

"Are you ready?" Theo asked, coming up beside her and offering her a hand. "You kind of look like you're casing the joint."

Meg laughed and grabbed his hand, squeezing it. "I am, in a way."

He raised his eyebrows, but then just grinned and shook his head. "I'm not even going to ask."

Inside the restaurant, she gave her name to the hostess, who informed them they'd need to wait a few minutes for their table. They sat down on a long bench to the right of the front door, giving Meg a prime view of the wait staff as they exited and entered the kitchen carrying circular trays of food, drink, or used dishes. She'd worked in the industry for so long that observing the inner workings of a restaurant as an outsider felt oddly voyeuristic. She couldn't take her eyes off of them, fascinated by their well-choreographed movements as they wove around patrons and co-workers alike.

She looked over at Theo, suddenly realizing that she'd been ignoring him for several minutes. He was engrossed in his phone, so she returned to people-watching. In the kitchen, something metal clanged to the floor and she winced. The telltale crash of glass or metal objects anywhere in a restaurant were never good, but even that interruption didn't faze the staff.

"Briggs, party of two," the hostess called out. Meg tore her attention away from the kitchen with reluctance.

Theo slipped the cell phone into the pocket of his pants. "Ready?"

She nodded, and they followed the hostess to a table on the outside deck.

"This is nice." Theo pulled out a chair and gestured for her to sit.

"Thanks." She flashed him a smile. It had surprised her the first time Theo had helped her into her seat at a restaurant, but now she appreciated his thoughtfulness. She sat, then looked around. He was right. The restaurant hadn't looked like much from the parking lot, but the massive cedar deck overlooking the river was impressive.

Planter boxes interspersed along the railing contained flowers that lightly scented the air. Wrought iron tables shaded by red canvas umbrellas dotted the deck's surface. Below, the river bubbled softly as it made its way out to Puget Sound. The overall effect was enchanting. She turned back to face Theo. "Wow. I like this a lot."

"Me too," he said absentmindedly, as he reached for one of the menus the hostess had left with them and turned his attention to the food selections.

He didn't seem nearly as impressed with the restaurant as she was, but then again, he was there for the food, not a reconnaissance mission. She surveyed the seating area. Almost all of the patrons were talking and laughing as they ate. No wonder this place received so many positive online reviews. She swallowed a lump that had formed in her throat. It wouldn't be easy to achieve the same thing when they opened the restaurant at the Inn.

Theo placed his menu on the table and sipped from the glass of wine that had appeared only a few minutes after he'd ordered it, right after they'd been greeted by their waitress. "You okay?"

She tried to smile, but her lips quivered.

"What's wrong?"

She gestured to their surroundings. "They've done such a great job here. I don't know if I can pull off the same thing at the Inn."

"I'm sure you'll be fine." He smiled, but his tone was dismissive. He pointed at her menu. "Did you decide what to order yet? Our waitress will be back soon."

"Uh, no. Not yet." She would have liked to discuss the apprehension she was feeling about starting a new restaurant, but he didn't seem interested in doing so. She grabbed the menu and selected the first thing that appealed to her: a plank-grilled salmon and a side of asparagus with a balsamic reduction.

The waitress reappeared as soon as Meg set her menu down on the table. "Hello," she said. "My name is Paula. Have you decided what you'd like, or do you need a little more time?"

"I think we're ready." Theo grinned up at her. "I'm going to have the ten-ounce sirloin." He gave the waitress the particulars, then Meg relayed her order. When she was finished, he added, "Oh, and we're celebrating her birthday tonight. Do you have anything special for dessert?"

Paula beamed at them. "We certainly do. I'll make sure to bring out our special complimentary birthday dessert after you've completed your main course."

"That would be wonderful." He smiled at her again. "Thank you so much, Paula."

She blushed slightly and nodded. "It's my pleasure."

She spun around and walked quickly back into the restaurant.

Meg stared at Theo. "My birthday isn't until February."

He shrugged. "I know, but they don't know that." He reached for her hand. "You seemed a little down tonight, so I thought you could use some cheering up."

Her stomach flip-flopped. On one hand, she didn't like lying to the restaurant staff. On the other, it had been a thoughtful gesture on his part and showed that, while he wasn't terribly interested in her concerns about her planned restaurant, he'd picked up on the stress she was experiencing.

She forced herself to smile. "Thanks."

"No problem."

They chatted for about thirty minutes until the food arrived. After a delicious dinner that lived up to the wonderful reviews, the waitress brought out a small chocolate lava cake topped with vanilla ice cream, and two spoons. A red candle perched atop it like a lighthouse, signaling to everyone that it was supposedly Meg's birthday. The flame flickered as several other members of the waitstaff joined their waitress at the table to sing a slightly off-key rendition of Happy Birthday. Meg's face burned. By the end of the song, she was sure her cheeks glowed as brightly as the candle.

They left, and Theo burst into laughter. "You should see yourself. You were pressed so tightly against your chair that I thought you'd disappear into it."

Meg glared at him and took a deep breath, then reminded herself he was only trying to cheer her up. "I'm not big on public attention."

He waved a hand in the air. "Eh, it wasn't a big deal."

He took one of the spoons and held it over the dessert. "Are you willing to share?"

Meg sighed. "Of course." She picked up her own spoon and sampled the rich chocolate cake mixed with just the right amount of creamy, vanilla bean-specked ice cream. By anyone's standards, it was excellent, but she couldn't eat more than a few bites.

"You don't like it?" Theo gestured to the cake.

"I liked it. I'm just full." Her face had cooled, but her stomach was still unsettled from all of the attention on her fake birthday. "Go ahead and take the rest if you want."

His eyes widened and he reached for the plate. "I'm not going to pass up that offer."

She leaned back in her chair, trying to enjoy the beautiful evening. The sun hung low in the sky but wouldn't set for over an hour. The puffy clouds floating above it would make for a breathtaking sunset over the bay.

She straightened in her seat. "Hey, do you want to see the barn at the Inn?" For some reason, in all the time they'd been dating, she'd never shown him the barn. Once he saw it, he'd have a better understanding of what she was trying to do with the place.

He looked up from a spoonful of melting ice cream. "The one you're going to turn into a restaurant?" He shrugged. "I guess so."

They finished their meal and drove back to Willa Bay. Meg pulled into a space in the Inn's parking lot and twisted the key to shut off the car. She turned to give Theo a faint smile, suddenly afraid of what he would think of the barn. Why hadn't she shown it to him before? Had she been too busy, or was it because she was afraid to find out what he thought about her dream?

He looked at her and returned her smile. "Okay, let's see this future restaurant of yours."

They exited the car, and she led him around the Inn and along the path leading to the barn. When it came into sight, Meg paused and looked up at it. In the waning daylight, the massive structure appeared even more decrepit than usual. She glanced at Theo to gauge his reaction.

He didn't bother to hide his disdain. With raised eyebrows, he asked, "This is the building you've been talking about?"

Meg's heart sank deep into her chest. "Yes," she said softly. "This is it."

Theo took a good, long look at the siding and whistled. "With how much you've talked this place up, I kind of expected it to be in better shape." He held his hand up to his forehead, shading his gaze from the last rays of the sun to scrutinize the broken windowpanes high above them.

"Did you want to see the inside?" Meg asked. She wasn't sure she wanted to find out his reaction to the interior of the barn, but they were already there, and she was hoping to make the best of it. Plus, maybe if she described to him exactly what she envisioned, he would see it too.

She slid open the barn door and flipped on the lights, illuminating piles of junk. Theo leaned against the entryway, his eyes wide as he took it all in. In that instant, Meg saw it exactly as he did.

They stood in a trash-filled building that could fall down at any time. She wouldn't have been surprised if he was thinking that it *should* be torn down. She wanted to show him where the kitchen would be, and tell him her vision for the dining room, but from the look on his face he wouldn't believe any of it.

"So, you're planning on having a restaurant in here?" he asked.

"Uh huh." She searched his expression, hoping to see a glimmer of hope or excitement for her. Unfortunately, there was none.

"It's great, babe." He moved behind her and squeezed her shoulders. "I'm sure that someday this place will be a real showpiece." He may have chosen those words specifically with the intent of sounding positive, but they didn't conceal the heavy doubt in his voice.

"Thanks." Meg leaned against him, hoping that the feel of his warm chest against her back would quell the waves of anxiety pulsing through her body. Was she crazy to think that she could turn this place into a restaurant? She turned and kissed him lightly on the lips. "Thanks for coming to see it."

She grabbed his hand, led him out of the barn, and shut the door behind them. As the lock clicked into place, she felt an odd sense of remorse, like her negative thoughts had been disloyal to the old building.

"Did you want to take a walk on the beach?" he asked.

She shook her head. "Not tonight. I'm getting a headache and should probably go lay down before it gets worse." Ordinarily, she would've liked nothing better than to take an evening stroll along the bay, but his reaction to the barn had confirmed her worst fears. If Theo had reservations about the feasibility of turning it into a restaurant, Zoe and Shawn must as well.

Meg drove Theo back to the marina and idled in the drop-off zone. He gave her a quick peck on the mouth, then got out of the car and walked jauntily toward the ramp to the docks, whistling a little tune that floated to her through her open window.

He acted like he didn't have a care in the world, and she doubted he understood how much his lackluster response to the barn had hurt her. She'd had fun during the first part of their date, but was merely enjoying each other's company enough to sustain a relationship? She'd always imagined having a partner who would share in her hopes and dreams, and support her through both good times and bad. At the very least, she wished he would take the lead once in a while and surprise her by planning an outing or two.

They hadn't dated for long, so maybe those qualities would develop as their romance matured. But what if they didn't? As the top of Theo's head disappeared below street level, she felt more unsure about everything than she had in months.

2

Taylor

Taylor Argo edged the metal spatula under the crispy skin of a pink salmon filet and slid it onto a plate. He took a second to admire the grill marks on the fish and how sharply they contrasted with the classic white plates used in the dining room of the Willa Bay Lodge. Elegant and simple—exactly the type of cuisine he was known for.

Brandon, the new sous-chef hired to replace Meg when she left, moved in sync with Taylor, plucking the plate from the counter to add the roasted root vegetables and rice pilaf to the dinner special. He set the fish entrée next to another on the warming countertop.

Brandon wasn't Meg, but he was working out.

Taylor had just flipped a chicken breast to its other side when he heard a woman tentatively clearing her throat behind him. He turned to see Kaley, one of the part-time waitresses who worked the dinner shift.

"Excuse me. Taylor?" Her voice was so timid that he

had to strain to hear her over the hissing meat on the grill and the pot of pasta boiling on the stove. She shifted her weight from foot to foot, her face contorted with worry.

This didn't look like something that could wait. Taylor glanced back at the grill to assess its contents. Nothing was in danger of burning, so he turned his full attention to the teenager standing a few feet away.

"Is everything okay?" he asked. Kaley was a newer member of their staff, but she'd acclimated quickly and didn't seem prone to panicking unnecessarily. Besides, it was just after five o'clock, and they'd only had a few guests so far.

"Um, sorry to bother you, it's just that some of the customers are asking about dessert." She held up the tall, narrow dessert menu he'd printed out earlier in the day.

"Okay?" He cocked his head to the side. "I'm not sure I understand the problem."

She took a deep breath. "We don't have anything to offer them for dessert. I can't find anything that's on the menu."

He stared at her. "That's impossible." He strode toward the walk-in refrigerator and yanked open the door, certain he'd be able to locate what their pastry chef had made earlier in the day. "Lara made mini cheesecakes and blackberry pie before she left. She was supposed to make some mousse too." He scanned the shelves of the walk-in. His confidence sank as his gaze slid over each item that wasn't one of the desserts on the menu. He spun on his heels. "Where are all of the desserts?"

Kaley shrank back, and Brandon poked his head around Taylor to see into the refrigerator too. "I saw Lara put something in there while I was prepping the salad greens earlier, but it looked more like a big cake than a pie or mini cheesecakes."

He stepped out of the way, and Taylor shut the heavy door before looking at each of them in turn. "Did either of you see Lara make any desserts for the Lodge before she left?"

They shook their heads in tandem.

"Nope." Brandon stared at the stainless-steel door. "I just figured she made them before I got here."

"She was gone before I arrived." Kaley's eyes were as wide as the saucers for the espresso they served with dessert. "Does this mean we don't have anything to give to the guests?"

"That's what it's looking like." Taylor's sense of calm was rapidly dissipating. He was at the end of his rope with Lara, but maybe there was a logical explanation for why they couldn't find any desserts. "Okay, give me a few minutes to find out what's going on." Taylor told Brandon to man the grill and excused himself to his office, shutting the door and leaning back in the chair to take a few deep breaths before picking up the phone to call Lara.

It rang four times before she finally answered, her voice bright. "Hello, this is Lara."

"Lara. It's Taylor." His voice was brittle, even to his own ears. He counted to five before continuing. "Where are the desserts for this evening?"

A pregnant pause followed. "Oh. I didn't actually make any. I had a cake that I needed to get to a client tonight and I didn't have time for the Lodge desserts."

"You didn't have time?" His brain was spinning. "Lara, that's your job. You make the pastries and sweets for the Lodge."

He could almost see her shrug as she answered, "I didn't have time. I'm sure there's something else you can give the guests tonight. I made plenty of cookies for the front desk and there's some ice cream in the freezer."

"You want me to feed them cookies for dessert?" She had to be kidding. The Lodge wasn't five-star rated, but it was well-regarded throughout the area and had a reputation to keep up.

"Yeah, why not? Everyone loves my peanut butter cookies." Voices murmured in the background on Lara's side and she was quiet, then came back on the line. "Listen Taylor, I've really got to go. I'll make sure to do the desserts tomorrow, okay?"

She hung up before he could inform her that it was most definitely not okay. He closed his eyes and rubbed at the ache in his jaw from gritting his teeth during their conversation. The Lodge's former pastry chef, Cassie, had always been the consummate professional, even though, like Lara, she'd also had a cake decorating business on the side. But Lara thought that just because her father owned the Lodge, she could pull a stunt like this.

His stomach clenched. It was times like this that he really missed the camaraderie he'd had with Meg. She'd always known how to calm him down—although, ironically, her own run-in with Lara had caused her to quit her job at the Lodge and go to work full-time at the resort she'd recently purchased with some friends. Four months ago, his life had been much different, before he'd ever heard of the Inn at Willa Bay or met Lara Camden. Unfortunately, there was no going back in time, and he had a restaurant to run.

He stood so suddenly that his chair careened across the plastic mat protecting the Berber carpet under his desk and hit the wall behind it. He took a deep breath and pushed the chair back in place. He'd figure out a solution to this problem—he always did.

His first stop was the walk-in freezer. Lara was right, there were several tall cartons of ice cream on the shelves.

He frowned as he read each of the labels: Chocolate Cherry Cheesecake, Mint Chocolate Chip, and Orange Sherbet. If all Lara had made were peanut butter cookies, none of these would pair well. Still, they could offer scoops of ice cream à la carte. It was better than nothing.

He shut the freezer door and strode back out into the middle of the kitchen where Kaley and Brandon were talking in hushed tones.

Kaley looked up, her eyes filled with hope. "Did you find anything?"

He shook his head. "No." He fought hard to keep the anger out of his voice, but couldn't keep a small amount from leaking through. "There was a miscommunication and she didn't make the desserts for tonight."

Kaley's face fell. Missing desserts didn't sound like a major issue, but it was one of the things the Lodge was famous for. A large part of Kaley's income came from tips, so with a lower bill for dinner and disgruntled customers, her nightly earnings were at stake. Taylor sighed. He hated to let her or their guests down.

But what was he going to do? Desserts suitable for a fine dining establishment couldn't just be pulled out of the air. Taylor surveyed the kitchen, his gaze landing on blocks of baking chocolate Lara had left out at the baker's station. "Okay, here's what we're going to do." He looked directly at Brandon. "Can you make a chocolate mousse?"

Brandon nodded. "Of course. One of the first things I learned in culinary school."

Taylor snapped his fingers. "Perfect. Please make a batch of it and think about how we can jazz it up a little." He turned to Kaley. "Let the guests know we have a special chocolate mousse and some wonderful, locally made ice cream on the menu tonight."

Doubt clouded her expression. "Okay, but I'm not sure that's going to be enough."

"It'll have to be for now." Taylor had an idea, but he wasn't sure if it would work. He jogged over to the grill and removed the fully-cooked meat. Brandon stood by his side, ready to take the plates over to his workspace. "Brandon, can you take over for thirty minutes? It shouldn't be too busy until later in the evening."

"Sure, no problem." The sous-chef's eyes were bright with curiosity, but he didn't ask any questions.

Taylor jogged over to his office and hung up his chef's jacket on the hook behind the door, then rushed out to the parking lot. He jangled his keys, considering his options. It was only five-thirty, so both the local fine-foods market and the Sea Star Bakery would still be open. The bakery would be more likely to have what he needed, but he wasn't sure how much inventory they'd have left this late in the day.

He decided to take his chances on the bakery. Fate must have been smiling down on him, because not only did he find a parking space only a few stores down, but the glass display case inside bulged with baked goods. The dining area was empty, with the exception of Cassie's son, Jace, who was chewing on the eraser of a pencil as he focused on a piece of paper bearing what appeared to be math problems.

"Hey, Taylor," Cassie called out from behind the counter. "What are you doing here? Is everything okay at the Lodge?"

"Yes," he answered automatically, then frowned. "I

mean, no. Things are not going well. Lara decided it wasn't important to make desserts for this evening at the restaurant." He probably shouldn't have told Cassie about his troubles with an employee, but at this point, he didn't really care who knew.

Cassie's eyes widened and her lips formed a silent "Oh". "She didn't make anything?" she said in a stage whisper as he neared the counter.

"Nope. Nothing." He trained his eyes on the display case, but thinking about Lara's unperturbed attitude regarding the whole mess made his vision blur with rage. The baked goods swam in front of him, their tantalizing aromas reminding him that he'd forgotten to eat dinner. After working in kitchens for so many years, he was used to smelling food all day, and had trained himself to work long shifts without a break. However, with this snafu, his defenses were down and now he could add hangry to his list of woes. "I need to buy something to serve. What do you suggest?"

"Hmm." Cassie squatted down to look through the display case, her face distorted behind the curved glass. She grabbed a tray from the bottom and popped back up. "What about these mini cheesecakes? I'm still trying to figure out how much to make of everything, so I have a lot of these left over today." She held up a raspberry-topped cheesecake in a ribbed foil wrapper. "What do you think?"

Taylor stared at the treat, mesmerized by the streaks of pink and red marbling the creamy surface. They looked amazing. Better than amazing. She'd made exactly what he'd asked Lara to bake. What were the odds? "I'll take them."

"How many do you want?" Cassie's hand hovered over the tray.

"All of them," Taylor said, rapidly calculating in his head how many customers they normally had on a Wednesday night in the summer. Way more than the three containers of ice cream could satisfy.

"I've got more in the back if you need them." She furrowed her brow and peered into the case. "What about the berry pies? Could you use those?"

He looked at her solemnly. "Cassie, you're a lifesaver. Thank you."

She blushed and grabbed a box from behind the counter. "I should be thanking you. I wasn't sure what I was going to do with all of these." She stacked the cheesecakes two-deep in a box with a thin layer of cardboard in between, then disappeared into the back room. A few minutes later, she returned with two more closed boxes and set all of them on top of the counter.

The bells over the front door jingled and they both looked in that direction.

Cassie waved at the newcomer. "Hey, Meg. After I finish ringing up Taylor, I'll get the kids ready to go with you. I can't even tell you how much Kyle and I appreciate you taking them for a few hours tonight. It's been a long time since we've had a dinner date alone."

"No problem." Meg sidled up to the counter, raising an eyebrow at the number of boxes. "How hungry are you, Taylor? Cassie's stuff is good, but this will take you a year to get through."

He chuckled, and some of the tension melted out of his shoulders. He hadn't run into Meg in a while and seeing her brightened his day. "It's for the Lodge."

"Lara forgot to make the desserts for tonight." Cassie didn't even try to hide the glee in her voice, reminding Taylor of how much she disliked Lara.

"Seriously?" Meg shook her head. "I bet she had some lousy excuse for it too."

"She had to finish and deliver a cake for her side business." Taylor handed Cassie his credit card. He'd get reimbursed by the Lodge, but the total still made him cringe.

"Typical." Meg glanced at Jace, then returned her attention to Taylor. "It looks like the little guy's pretty into his homework, so I've got a few minutes. Do you want some help carrying everything out to your car?"

"Sure." He flashed her a grin. "I've got to get back to the Lodge quickly, so I wouldn't turn down an offer of help."

After everything was bagged up, Taylor and Meg grabbed as much as they could carry and headed for the exit.

Cassie beat them to the door and held it open for them. "Sorry I can't help. I don't want to leave the bakery unattended."

"No worries," Taylor said. "I really do appreciate getting all of these."

"Yeah, well make sure people know where they came from." Cassie scrunched up her face as though she'd bit into a sour lemon. "I don't want people giving Lara credit for them."

He laughed. "I'll make sure to add the bakery's name before each item when I type up the selections." They'd have to quickly redo the dessert menus when he got back to the Lodge, anyway, and it wouldn't take much more effort to credit the Sea Star Bakery. Although Cassie had taken over from a previous bakery in the same location, she still had to prove her own baking skills to the town, and he was happy to help her do so.

When he and Meg were safely out on the sidewalk with their loads, Cassie let the door swing closed behind them.

"Where'd you park?" Meg asked, squinting into the sunlight.

"Up the street, in front of Johnson's Antiques." He led the way, with her following closely behind him. He placed the boxes on his sedan's trunk while he unlocked the car and opened the back passenger door. After positioning his desserts on the seat, he reached for Meg's bags. Their fingers touched as his hands closed around the handle of the plastic sack, sending tingles up his arm. Her eyes flickered to his face. Had she felt it too? She smiled, and he thought he might drop the bags.

Instead, he gripped them tighter and moved away from her to settle them into the car. As he turned back around, he said, "Looks like we should have room for everything. I don't think there were too many more to bring out."

She nodded, and bit her lower lip. "How's everything going at the Lodge since I left? I haven't heard from you in a while."

He was silent for a few seconds as they moved around a couple who were partially blocking the sidewalk, strolling along with their arms looped around each other. "Things are mainly okay. The new sous-chef, Brandon, seems like a good guy."

"And Lara?" She peered at him.

A flash of irritation ran through him, not at Meg's question, but at the situation back in the kitchen. "Lara is Lara."

"That bad?" Her words were thick with sympathy.

He stopped walking and ran his hands over his gelled hair. "Yeah. I mean, they're not great. Most days aren't too bad, but she's still making huge messes in the kitchen and expecting everyone else to clean up after her. And, well, you know what happened today." His breath came out in a loud whoosh, and he locked eyes with Meg. "I need to talk to George again. She may be his daughter, but she technically reports to me, and I can't have this happening in my kitchen."

Meg briefly touched his arm, so softly that he wasn't entirely sure he hadn't imagined it. "I'm sorry, Taylor. I wish I could have stayed at the Lodge. At least then we could hate her together."

He gave her a small smile. "I'm glad you quit. I hated seeing you so unhappy."

"I wouldn't say working at the Lodge was the reason I wasn't happy." She started walking again and he had to quicken his pace to catch up.

"What was it, then?" He'd wanted to ask her before, but things had happened so fast after she'd quit, and he'd had to focus on hiring new staff to replace her.

They'd reached the bakery, but she stopped outside the door, regarded him thoughtfully, then shrugged. "I don't know. It seemed like everyone else had wonderful new opportunities in their lives, but mine wasn't changing at all. Zoe had Shawn and the Inn to focus on and Cassie opened her own bakery. I was still working at the same old job I had been at for the last two years."

"You have a lot of good things in your life though, with the Inn and that guy you were dating. Are you still with him?" He held his breath, half wishing she'd tell him they'd broken up.

"Yeah, Theo and I are still together," she said, dashing his hopes. She sighed dramatically before continuing, "I know. I should be happy with everything I do have. Maybe it was just Lara coming back to town that set me off?" Her eyes twinkled with mirth. "There's something about her that gets under everyone's skin." She leaned against the side of the building and traced a scar in the concrete sidewalk with the toe of her sneaker. "I'm just feeling a little out of sorts, that's all. I'm helping out at the Inn, but I won't have much of my own there until we get the restaurant up and running."

"When will that be?"

Her face darkened, and he wondered if he'd said something wrong. Finally, she said, "I don't know—maybe never."

What was she talking about? The last time he'd spoken with her, she'd sounded excited about the prospect of turning the barn into a restaurant. He immediately wanted to press her for more details, but allowed her room to continue.

She sighed deeply, her eyes troubled. "If it works out, maybe by January. But it's going to take a lot of hard work to pull that off. If I can't get the barn cleared out by October, Shawn will have to move on to a different project."

"Is there anything I can do to help?" The words shot out of his mouth before he'd had a chance to think them through. He wanted to help Meg, but he'd been trying to keep his distance from her. He'd always felt a pull of attraction between the two of them, but he hadn't felt right pursuing anything with her while she worked for him. Besides, she'd never given him any indication that she shared his feelings, and now she had a boyfriend. To avoid any awkwardness, it was best to keep their friendship on a more casual level.

Meg put her hand on the door handle, then stared up at the sky thoughtfully. "I could use some assistance clearing out the old barn. I've done a little, but there are things in there I can't move by myself, like rusty old farm machinery and heavy wooden furniture. Zoe and Shawn are so caught up in getting everything ready for guests at the Inn that they don't have time to help me." She laughed self-deprecatingly. "But I'm sure you don't want to get involved with that grungy task, any more than anyone else does. Besides, I know how busy you are with the restaurant, especially with all of the new staff."

Before he could respond, she pushed the door open and stalked over to the counter to grab a few more bags filled with square bakery boxes. He trailed behind her. She'd given him an out, but should he take it? He *was* busy, so if he told her he didn't have time to help her, it wouldn't be a lie. Still, it didn't feel right to back out on his offer.

After Cassie had them both loaded like sherpas carrying gear up Mt. Everest, Meg jetted out of the bakery, racing along the sidewalk toward his car. He rushed after her, almost tripping over a woman who'd stopped to pet a dog. With the number of boxes he was holding, he was grateful for his long arms and over six feet of height. It would have been difficult to see over what he was holding if he'd been any shorter.

When he got to his car, Meg was leaning against it, waiting for him. "It's about time," she joked.

"Hey," he said. "I got stuck behind some pedestrians." He followed the same maneuver he'd performed with the prior load to stow everything away in his car.

While he was securing the last box, Meg said, "Well, good luck with Lara and everything." She turned to leave.

"Wait." He straightened up and shut the car door, then stepped back onto the sidewalk. "I'd be happy to help with the barn."

"Really?" Her eyes glittered with hope, and his

stomach dropped to his knees. He'd just offered to spend a whole day alone with Meg, knowing full well that she was still involved with someone else.

He nodded. "Sure. When do you want me to come over? Mondays and Tuesdays are best, since the restaurant's closed. I'll be able to help for a full day."

"I'll check my calendar and let you know." Her tone had lightened, and she bounced slightly on the balls of her feet as she spoke. "Thank you so much." To his surprise, she crossed the short distance between them and wrapped her arms around him.

His heart beat faster. She was so close that the fruity scent of her shampoo tickled his nose. He held his breath, torn between not wanting the embrace to end and an intense desire to run away in fear. He patted her back awkwardly a few times.

She stepped away from him, her face flushed. "Sorry. I got a little carried away. I can't even tell you how much it means to me that you're willing to help."

"No worries." He shot her what he hoped was a breezy smile and crossed to the other side of the car to put some space between them. He swung the ring of keys against his leg as he spoke to her over the roofline. "Give me a call when you figure out when you want to clean the barn."

"I will." She waved at him. "Good luck with Lara and everything."

He watched her walk back to the bakery, her dark hair swinging behind her in a long ponytail as she strode along the sidewalk. He got into the car and sat behind the wheel for a few minutes. Although he'd been saddened by Meg's decision to leave her job at the Lodge, he'd understood why she'd needed to do so. Plus, her departure had offered the benefit of not having to see her every day and tell himself he didn't have any feelings for her. Now, by volunteering to help with the barn, he'd put himself in a position where he'd be spending vast amounts of time alone with her. He turned the key in the ignition and the car roared to life.

So much for good intentions.

3

DEBBIE

"Grandma, would you like some more tea?" Kaya asked, holding a child-sized, pink-and-purple plastic teapot up in the air.

Debbie Briggs pushed a tiny cup that matched the teapot across the table until it rested directly in front of her youngest granddaughter. "Why, thank you," she said in an exaggerated manner. "I'd love some more tea." She pointed to the stuffed bunny with mottled white, black, and gray fur perched between the two of them in her own chair. "Do you think Little Bunny would like some too?"

Kaya solemnly regarded her favorite stuffie. "I think she's had enough for today." She held her hand up to the side of her mouth, as if to shade it from the rabbit's view. "Sometimes she has potty accidents if she drinks too much."

"Ah." Debbie nodded just as solemnly, pressing her lips together tightly to keep her laughter from spilling out. "I see."

Kaya poured watered-down tea into Debbie's cup and carefully slid it back across the table. She set the teapot on a lacy paper doily, looked forlornly at her empty plate, and then up at her grandmother. "Can I please have some more cookies?"

"Sure. Which ones do you want?"

"Uh." Kaya stared at the remaining cookies on the serving platter, her big blue eyes flickering with indecision. A few of the peanut butter and jelly and tuna salad sandwiches Debbie had made for the party sat on one half of a platter she'd borrowed for the occasion from her own set of wedding china. It wasn't something she'd serve clients of her catering company, but it suited her and Kaya just fine. The cookies, though, were always her granddaughter's favorite part of a tea party, no matter what kind she made.

Debbie flashed back to all of the tea parties she'd shared with her three girls when they were young. Kaya was the spitting image of her mother—Debbie's oldest daughter, Libby—when she was that age. Spending time with Kaya brought back so many good memories, and Debbie hoped someday her younger daughters, Meg and Samantha, would bless her with more grandchildren. That didn't seem like it would happen anytime soon, but she could still hope.

Kaya fixed her attention back on her grandma. "Can I have a chocolate chip cookie *and* a lemon bar?"

"Sure, honey." Debbie plucked the treats from the platter and set it on Kaya's plastic plate.

"Can Panda have one too?" Kaya asked hopefully a moment later, as she licked the last bit of lemon curd off of her fingers. "He loves lemon bars."

The slightly lopsided panda bear on her other side had a pitiful expression on his face and Debbie couldn't hold back a chuckle anymore. "I think Panda might get a little sticky if he ate one. Remember what happened when Paddington had those pastries?" She'd read the classic children's story to Kaya the last time the grandkids had spent the night.

Kaya regarded the stuffed animal, then said, "You're probably right. He hates baths, so that probably wouldn't be a good idea."

"Uh-huh." Debbie started stacking up their dishes. "Okay, honey. What do you want to do now? Maybe you could work on coloring in your pictures on Grandpa's birthday card while I load the dishwasher?"

"Okay, Grandma." Kaya grabbed her two stuffies and carried them over to the dining room table, which was half-covered by a large piece of butcher paper and about a hundred loose crayons. As soon as Libby had dropped Kaya off that morning, Kaya had insisted she needed to make a really big card for Grandpa's upcoming birthday. Debbie had helped her with the lettering, but the rest of it was all Kaya.

Debbie stood at the sink, washing their plates, her heart filling with each furtive glance at her granddaughter. Her family meant the world to her. When she'd been diagnosed with breast cancer two years ago, she'd wondered if she'd have the chance to see the little ones grow up. Now, with a clean bill of health from her oncologist a few months ago, she intended to make the most of her time with them and the rest of her family.

Years before her cancer diagnosis, after her kids had moved out of the house, Debbie had started her own catering business. Meg had opted to stay near the college she'd attended in Oregon to pursue a culinary career, but Libby had joined Debbie in her business, and Samantha, who worked full-time during the year as a physical education teacher at the local high school, helped out on occasion.

While Debbie was undergoing chemotherapy treatments, she and the girls had drastically reduced the number of catering jobs they'd accepted. Now that Debbie was better, Libby had hinted that she'd like to grow their business even more. Secretly, though, Debbie would much rather stay home and spend time with her grandkids.

But how could she say that to Libby? Libby had been her rock while she'd undergone treatments, driving her to appointments and helping her at home. Debbie's husband, Peter, had done what he could, but he worked full-time and wasn't around during the day. She wasn't sure what they would've done without Libby's help.

Debbie finished washing the last dish and set it in the wooden rack to dry. The sun shone through the window over the sink, and she turned her face up to enjoy its warmth. These were days worth remembering.

"Grandma?" Kaya's voice broke through Debbie's thoughts. "Want to see the card?"

"Definitely." Debbie dried her hands on the terrycloth hand towel hanging from the oven door and walked over to the dining room table. "Oh, honey, that's wonderful."

Kaya's chest swelled with pride. "I know. Grandpa's going to love it."

Debbie grinned at her. "He sure is." Kaya had folded over the length of butcher paper to form a card measuring about three feet by two feet. She'd drawn a birthday cake in the middle, surrounded by stick figures. "Can you tell me about it?"

Kaya stabbed her fingers at the thick paper. "That's a chocolate cake because Grandpa loves chocolate cake. And those are all of us in the family. You, Mommy, Daddy,

Auntie Meg, Auntie Samantha, and my sister and brothers." She giggled. "And me, of course. I'm the one next to Grandpa with the balloon."

"It's beautiful. Is it okay if I move it to somewhere safe until Grandpa's birthday?" Debbie lifted the corners of the card, considering the size of it. Where was she going to put this until the end of the month?

"I guess that's okay. But don't bend it," Kaya instructed.

"I won't." Debbie took it upstairs and opened the closet in her craft room. She still had an old portfolio holder in the back, and the card fit perfectly. Before leaving, Debbie hesitated for a moment in the middle of the room. Projects of all types covered the table and filled the bookshelves. She'd gotten back into crafting recently and couldn't wait to finish some of the things she'd started.

She closed the door so their cat wouldn't get in and wreak havoc, then came downstairs to find Kaya sitting on the living room floor playing with her stuffies. "Mommy will be here soon to pick you up after your brother's soccer game."

"Okay." Kaya hung her head, then looked up at Debbie. "Can I spend the night with you instead?"

Debbie cocked her head to the side. Although she knew Kaya loved hanging out with her grandmother, she was a mommy's girl and normally was excited when Libby came to get her. "What's the matter?"

Kaya rubbed the soft fur on Panda's leg. "Mommy seems mad a lot."

"Mad?" Debbie sat down next to Kaya and pulled her into her lap. This was definitely one thing that had been easier with her own kids. Being in her sixties now, she'd much rather sit in a chair than on the floor.

"She yells at us a lot, and she and Daddy are always

talking in their bedroom with the door closed." Kaya's lips quivered.

"Oh, honey, I'm sure she's not mad at you." Debbie stroked Kaya's silky hair and the little girl relaxed into her. She had noticed Libby seemed a little on edge lately, but she wasn't sure why. From snippets of conversations she'd overheard between her daughters and their friends, she'd learned Libby suspected Gabe might be cheating on her. It wasn't something Debbie would have expected from her son-in-law, but if life had taught her anything, it was that things didn't always go the way you hoped.

As if on cue, the doorbell rang.

"There's Mommy," Debbie said.

Kaya sprang from her lap and ran to the door, peering through the tall, frosted sidelight next to it. "Hi, Mommy."

"Hi, sweetie." Libby's voice was muffled as she pressed her face close to the window. Debbie opened the door and let Libby inside. Libby leaned down to hug Kaya. "How was your day at Grandma's?"

Kaya hugged her back, seemingly forgetting any concerns about her mother. "Good. I made a birthday card for Grandpa and we had a tea party." She scrunched up her face. "Don't worry, I didn't let Little Bunny have too much tea."

"Ah," Libby said knowingly. "Good thing." She moved past Kaya into the house.

"Would you like a cup of coffee?" Debbie asked.

Libby considered the offer, then shrugged. "Sure, I could use another cup. That was the longest soccer match ever. At least it wasn't raining, but the other kids were getting antsy and I was so happy for it to be over." She followed Debbie into the kitchen and sat down at the table.

Debbie brought two coffee cups over to where Libby

was sitting and took her usual seat at the head of the table. "If you'd like, I've got some leftover cookies from our tea party. I managed to keep Panda's paws off of the last lemon bar."

Libby laughed. "I do love your lemon bars, but I'm planning on starting dinner as soon as I get home." She rubbed the pad of her thumb against the curve of the mug's ceramic handle and stared into the cup.

"Something's bothering you." Debbie narrowed her eyes at her daughter. She'd given Libby space to work through her issues, but she was tired of being in the dark about what was going on in her own daughter's life. "What is it?"

Libby lifted her head and met Debbie's gaze. "I wanted to talk to you about taking on more catering jobs. I have a lead on a few weddings in the next couple of weeks. Maybe even some other, smaller events. You're feeling better, so we should jump on these opportunities when we can."

Now it was Debbie's turn to stare into her coffee. "I don't know. I was kind of enjoying spending time with the grandkids and getting back into some of my hobbies." Her eyes darted over to the basket next to her recliner where three skeins of yarn in different colors poked out. She'd made blankets for all of Libby's kids soon after they were born, but Kaya was four and Debbie still hadn't finished hers yet.

Libby grinned at her and shook her head dismissively. "Oh, Mom. You've got plenty of time for that. Think of how great this would be for us. It would be like old times."

The trouble was, Debbie wasn't sure she wanted to go back to the days when she wasn't home to get dinner ready and had no time to do the things she enjoyed.

"I don't know." She scanned Libby's face. "Have you

asked Samantha what she thinks?" Libby had obviously been under a lot of stress lately, and with four kids in extracurricular activities, she didn't have a lot of spare time for additional work. Debbie hadn't heard from Samantha in a few weeks, so it was unlikely she'd be interested in extra hours either.

Libby frowned. "I haven't heard from Sam in a while. It's like she dropped off the face of the earth. I called her last week, but just got voicemail."

Debbie's stomach twisted. Samantha had a tendency to disappear in the summer as she cobbled together odd jobs to make up for the break in her teacher's salary during those months. Still, it was unusual for her not to talk to anyone in the family. Since she wasn't returning phone calls, it was probably time to call Brant, Samantha's long-time boyfriend, and get an update on her daughter's life. Libby dabbed her face with a napkin, catching Debbie's attention.

"Is this what you want?" Debbie studied her daughter.

"It is. I need those extra jobs." Libby's voice cracked and her eyes glistened with unshed tears. "Mom. I have to tell you something about Gabe."

Debbie froze. Oh no. She'd hoped it wouldn't come to this. Her hands balled into fists under the table. "Is he... I mean, has he been...?" She stopped, unable to put her fears into words.

Libby's eyes widened. "No, no. It's not that. But it's not good news either. The company Gabe works for isn't doing very well and he expects they'll be handing out pink slips soon."

Debbie relaxed her fingers and exhaled deeply. Now it made sense why Libby would want to give up the little free time she had. More catering jobs meant more income, and with four little mouths to feed, they needed whatever money they could get. As much as Debbie would have loved to take it easy as she entered her retirement years, those were her grandkids, and this was her daughter sitting in front of her, pleading with her to take on more work.

"Oh, honey. I'm so sorry." Debbie leaned across the table and laid her hand on Libby's arm. "Does he have any prospects for a new job?"

Libby shook her head. "Not yet. His company has been so great to him over the last few years and he doesn't want to bail out on them until things are more certain. I told him he should start looking, but what can I say—he's loyal." A faint smile curved across her lips. "At least I know I have a good man."

"That you do." Debbie patted Libby's hand, then sat back and sipped her coffee. Thank goodness Libby and Gabe seemed to have patched up whatever had been troubling their relationship. She'd wager that the impending job loss had been a big factor in any marital stress, but she doubted she'd ever hear anything about it from Libby. Her eldest daughter liked to keep things to herself, even when doing so was detrimental to her own mental health.

But Debbie understood. It wasn't like she'd ever wanted to confide in her own mother about her relationship with Peter. Elizabeth Arnold and Debbie were as close as Debbie was to her own daughters, but there were some things that were better left unspoken.

"So, what do you think about catering more weddings?" Libby's face was full of hope and Debbie didn't want to let her down.

Debbie took a steadying sip of coffee, then let her lips ease into a smile. "I think we've got some weddings to bid on."

"Oh, thank you, Mama." Libby got up and wrapped her arms around Debbie. "I think this is going to be great for both of us. You'll get out of the house more, and the money will be good. Maybe you and Dad can finally take the trip to Europe you've always talked about."

Debbie hugged her back. She and Peter had been meaning to take a trip to Italy, but money hadn't been the biggest factor holding them back. Peter's job as a manager at a local manufacturer was time consuming. It seemed like every time they thought about planning a vacation, something went wrong at the plant and he was sucked back into working long hours.

Libby looked up at the yellow cat-shaped clock that had hung on the wall of Debbie's kitchen since Libby and her sisters were kids, then stood. "Kaya and I had better get home. I didn't realize how late it was already." She laughed. "I think we'll have spaghetti for dinner again. I never thought we'd eat so much spaghetti, but with the kids' sports schedules, I'm just glad to have something that's quick, cheap, and not McDonald's." She pushed her chair back under the table and walked across the kitchen to the dining room where Kaya was scribbling on a sheet of white printer paper. "Time to go, sweetie."

"Okay, Mommy." Kaya showed her what she'd been coloring. "See? I drew Grandma and me having a tea party." She held it out to Debbie. "It's for you, Grandma."

Debbie's heart melted as she crossed the room to take the paper from Kaya. "I'll treasure it always." She walked Kaya and Libby to the door, hugging them both tightly before they left.

When the door closed, Debbie took a closer look at the picture. Kaya had drawn a large red heart between the two figures. Debbie sat down at the kitchen table and ran her fingers over the waxy red heart. Taking on more catering jobs meant she'd have far less time with Kaya and the other kids. But, Libby needed her. Sometimes it seemed like being a mother meant sacrificing her own desires in favor of what was best for her children, but she wasn't sure she'd want it any other way.

4

SAMANTHA

Sam blew a few short blasts with her whistle. "No running around the pool," she shouted to two teenage boys racing each other to the deep end. They slowed to a rapid walk, but she had no doubt she'd soon be reprimanding them for trying to dive headfirst into the six-foot-deep water. Like most of the older kids at the massive pool located on the twelfth level of the Scenic Waves cruise ship, their parents were nowhere to be seen.

She sat back in the elevated lifeguard chair and scanned the water through the dark lenses of her sunglasses. There was a lively game of Marco Polo happening in the deep end. Over in the shallow end, toddlers wearing life jackets stood nervously on the pool steps while their parents coaxed them in with outstretched arms. The Caribbean sun beat down on her, warming her arms through the UV-protective sleeves of her zip-up uniform jacket. There were definitely worse places to be on a summer day.

She hadn't planned to work as a lifeguard over the summer, but when her friend, Miranda, had to cut her employment contract short when her mother fell seriously ill, the cruise line hadn't been able to find a replacement lifeguard on such short notice during the busy season. They'd asked Miranda if she knew anyone who'd qualify, and knowing that Samantha had worked as a lifeguard in the past, Miranda had recommended her for the temporary job.

As a PE teacher at Willa Bay High School, Samantha usually worked whatever jobs she could find over the summer to make ends meet until the school year started. Normally, she wouldn't have been so keen to travel halfway around the world on a moment's notice and leave behind her boyfriend, family, and friends, but this opportunity had given her the much-needed time and space to think about where her life was going.

Her reprieve from the real world would soon come to an end, however. Miranda's mother had made a full recovery and her friend was due back in a little over a week.

"Has it been pretty slow this afternoon?" A man in his early twenties asked from below. Samantha glanced at her watch and then down at him. "Is it three-thirty already?"

He laughed, pulling his sunglasses off his tanned face to clean them with the hem of the white t-shirt he wore over his red swim trunks. "Yep. You're free."

She climbed down from the chair and gave him a quick rundown on the issues she'd seen that day. "Have fun!" she said, flashing him a big smile as she walked away. She'd been working in the heat since the pool opened at seven that morning and all she wanted to do was grab a snack from the crew mess and flop lazily onto her bed to relax.

She picked up a bagel and cream cheese from the cafeteria and brought them back to her room. Her cabin mate, Kellie, was already there, kicked back on the lower bunk while she watched a movie on the TV affixed to the wall. When she saw Samantha enter, Kellie removed her headphones. "Hey."

"Hey." Samantha set the food on the small table that folded out from the wall and sat down to eat.

"Rough day?" Kellie asked.

"No, not really. It's weird, though, working every day without a break." She hadn't had a day off since she'd arrived on the ship and didn't expect to get one before she was relieved of her duties next week.

Kellie grinned. "You get used to it. I've been doing this for a few years, and I love it."

A chime came from the small cubby near the top bunk, where Samantha kept her cell phone. The cruise line didn't offer free internet to the crew, so she only accessed her messages while in port, like they were now. Samantha jumped to her feet and reached up to fish around for it in the compartment. She turned the phone over. One new e-mail. She opened it and returned to the table to read the message from her mom.

Where are you? I've called you over and over, but you don't answer. No one in the family has heard from you. Brant said you were fine, and just needed some space from everyone, but he wouldn't say why. I'm getting worried. Please call or e-mail me to let me know you're okay. Love, Mom.

Samantha's stomach rolled like the ship when it hit rough waters on the open seas. She hadn't meant to worry her family, but she hadn't been in a good place when she'd left Willa Bay. They all loved Brant, and they'd never understand why she'd had to break up with him.

The lifeguarding job had been a welcome distraction

and had provided her with a neutral place to work through her feelings about the breakup. Soon, though, it would be time to face her family and return to her normal life.

"You look stressed," Kellie observed. "Was it bad news?"

Samantha sighed and set her phone down on the tabletop. "No. Just my mom, wondering where I am."

Kellie's eyes widened. "You didn't tell her you were taking this job?"

"No." Samantha's eyes strayed back to the phone and her stomach clenched. "She would have been full of questions about where I was going, and I didn't want to get into the whole breakup thing with her before I left."

"She must be worried." Kellie slid off the bed and straightened the olive-green bedspread. After they'd roomed together for a week and become friends, Samantha had confided in her about what had happened with Brant. Having someone to talk to who was far removed from the situation had been helpful, allowing Samantha to work through some of her guilt and confusion.

"I know." Samantha slid the bagel back into the paper sack and stuck it in the small refrigerator tucked under the counter. "I'll e-mail her back while we're in port."

Kellie busied herself getting ready for her upcoming shift at the Kids Club. Samantha enjoyed her cabin mate's company, but after a long day at the pool, she was grateful for the chance to spend some quiet time alone. "Are you looking forward to going home?" Kellie asked as she fixed her hair and makeup, glancing at Samantha's reflection in the mirror.

"Yeah." Samantha folded the table back against the wall and pushed the wooden chair against it. Their cabin was of adequate size, but so compact that it was difficult to move around if they didn't keep it tidy. "I'm excited to head back to school and see all of my students."

"Do you like teaching?" Kellie asked. "I've been thinking about going back to college to finally finish my teaching degree. The Kids Club has reminded me how much I enjoy working with children."

"Yeah, I do." Samantha laughed, thinking about some of the students' antics. "Most of the time, at least. Last year, I taught one freshman English class and then a few sessions of PE. I usually also have to pick up some after-school sports to round out a full-time paycheck."

"I'm planning on teaching elementary school. Maybe upper elementary. I love how kids that age are figuring out who they are and what they're interested in." Kellie grabbed her sunglasses off of the dresser and stuck them on top of her head. "Do you want to grab dinner together at seven? I should have my lunch break then."

"Sounds good." Samantha eyed her bed. "I think I might grab some z's in the meantime. That sun just wipes me out."

Kellie laughed. "Oh yeah, you're from Washington State, huh. You're probably not used to the strong rays."

"Nope." Samantha joked, "Where I live, we tend to panic when we see the sun. We're not sure what to do with it." She pulled a pair of yoga pants and a tank top out of her drawer. "Have fun at work. I'll see you in a few hours." She headed into the tiny bathroom they shared as Kellie went out the door.

When she finished changing, Samantha climbed up onto the top bunk with her phone and stretched out on her stomach to return her mom's e-mail. She started to type, but then paused. Should she say anything to her family about breaking up with Brant? It wasn't like it would matter if she put off telling them the news, and she really didn't want to get into it while she was thousands of miles away in the middle of the ocean. The news would only make her mom worry more.

Hey,

I'm really sorry I didn't tell you where I was going. I got an opportunity to serve as a lifeguard aboard the Scenic Waves cruise ship and I jumped at the chance to try something new. I've been at sea most of the time, without phone or internet, but I should have contacted you to let you know I'm okay. The job is only temporary, and I'll be home in Willa Bay sometime next week.

Love you,

Sam

She'd told her mom a little white lie—she had been at sea for most of the time, but they'd stopped at a few ports where she could have e-mailed if she'd wanted to. But she'd also figured that they'd eventually call Brant and he'd tell them where she was. She hit send and watched the e-mail to her mother disappear from the screen. As she was stashing the phone back in her cubby, she heard the notification ping. *Well that was fast,* she thought. Her mom must have been waiting by the computer for her to respond.

It wasn't an e-mail from her mother though—it was something from work. Samantha clicked on the e-mail from the Willa Bay School District and quickly skimmed it. Her heart hammered as she read the words, "not renewing your contract". She carefully read the e-mail a second time. Apparently, the school district was low on funds and they'd had to make the difficult decision to cut back on physical education programs and some after-school sports. As such, her services wouldn't be needed for the upcoming school year.

She blinked a few times and set the phone down on her mattress, the bright screen still reflecting her notice of termination. She lay back, her head hitting the pillow with a muffled thud, and stared at the plain white ceiling about three feet above her bunk.

Now what? Her temporary job was ending in a week and she would be returning home, but to what? Her long-term relationship with Brant was over and she no longer had a job that she loved. A few months ago, she'd been engaged to a man she thought she'd marry and working at the same school she'd taught at since graduating from college. In the space of a few weeks, all that had evaporated.

She closed her eyes, hoping sleep would come to her, but worries about the future raced through her brain. How was she going to pay the rent on her apartment? Or buy food? Or get health insurance? She was going to have to locate another job as soon as she returned to Willa Bay, but what were the odds of finding another teaching position a few weeks before the school year started?

One thing was for sure—she dreaded telling her family they'd been right about her all along. Until she'd taken the job at the high school and met Brant, she'd been the baby of the family, the one who couldn't seem to get—or keep—her life together. Now, in the space of a month, she was back to square one, struggling to find her place in the world.

5

Meg

Meg leaned back in the cushioned chair on the Inn's front porch and rested her feet on the edge of the coffee table. A Thermos full of coffee, two mugs, and a box of pastries from the Sea Star Bakery sat on the end table next to her. The Inn had been bustling over the past weekend, hosting two large weddings. They wouldn't be offering overnight accommodations until after the grand opening at the end of the month, however, so at eight o'clock on a Tuesday morning, Meg had the place to herself.

Boats dotted the serene surface of the bay, captained by fishermen who had probably been out on the water long before her alarm had gone off that morning. Meg hadn't entered the Inn, but she could hear Celia bustling around inside. Zoe and Shawn lived in cottages on the premises, but neither of them had made an appearance yet.

A sedan crunched over the gravel in the driveway and rolled to a stop in front of the house.

"Is it okay to park here?" Taylor called out the window.

Meg pointed to a short driveway about forty feet away that led to a gravel parking lot. "You can park in there. I don't think there are any events today, but better safe than sorry."

He nodded in understanding and moved his car. When she saw his tall form walking back toward her, Meg grabbed everything off of the table, hooking her left index finger through the handles of the mugs so she wouldn't drop them.

He met her on the lawn in front of the porch and nodded at the yellow box she held in her hands. "Great minds think alike."

Until he'd said something, she hadn't even noticed the white box he was holding.

"Are those donuts from A Hole in One?" she asked, eying the box. She'd been craving donuts, but had decided it was better to support Cassie's bakery. Not that Meg minded the absence of donuts—her friend was an amazing baker and had yet to make something that Meg hadn't loved.

"Yep, they sure are. Here, let me help you." Taylor flashed her a bright smile and took the other box from her, stacking it on top of his.

"Thanks."

He looked around and whistled. "Wow, you guys have done a great job on this place."

Her heart swelled with pride. "Thanks. It was mainly Shawn and Zoe, but I helped a bit too."

"So, where's the barn?" he asked, craning his neck around. "I don't remember seeing it before."

"It's on the other side of the property and kind of blocked from view by a stand of trees. Are you ready to get started?"

49

He nodded. "I've been curious to see the barn after hearing you talk about it so much."

Her cheeks warmed. She'd probably been blabbing about it and her future restaurant far more than any of her friends had ever wanted to hear. "Sorry."

He stopped. "No, I'm serious. I really want to see it. It sounds interesting."

She checked his face for signs that he was patronizing her, but didn't see any. After the disappointment she'd experienced when showing the barn to Theo, she had no illusions that other people would see it the same way she did.

"It's over here." She led him to the path down to the old barn. The peeling paint, shattered windowpanes, and rotting shingles were painfully apparent in the harsh light of the morning sun. She slid the door open, then stepped aside to allow Taylor room to view the interior.

He strode past her, as if eager to get inside. Sunlight streamed through broken windows, catching dust motes dancing in the air. He paused in the middle of the hay-strewn main floor and surveyed the interior, zeroing in on the stalls.

"How many horses did they have at the resort back then?" he asked.

She shrugged, loosening some of the tension in her shoulders. "I'm not sure. I think most of the stalls were for horses that the guests brought, but the Inn did have a few of their own for guests to ride on the beach." She watched as he slowly turned a full circle, taking a painfully long time to see the barn in its entirety.

His gaze landed on the ladder to the loft. "Can we go up there?" he asked.

"Sure." She led him over to it and stepped on the bottom rung. "Shawn said the ladder is sound, but just to be on the safe side, wait until I'm at the top before you come up, okay?" She stashed the coffee mugs and Thermos in her vintage fabric hobo bag, hoping nothing would break or spill as she climbed. The satchel she'd bought at a flea market in Portland was one of her most prized possessions. It was like a Mary Poppins bag, seeming to expand to hold everything she could possibly need.

Taylor nodded, and she climbed to the top. While he followed her up, balancing the two bakery boxes with the agility of a monkey, she took a quick look down into the barn. Somehow, the objects stored below looked even worse from here. A thick layer of dirt or dust covered everything, and from this angle, all of the odds and ends that had been crammed in behind the larger items were visible. There was no way he'd be able to see her vision for the barn in this mess. Even Zoe and Shawn, who both had a strong passion for restoring the Inn to its former glory, were skeptical of her dream.

He reached the top, situated himself near the edge, and let his legs swing loosely in midair. Just thinking about doing that made her queasy. She sat down next to him, a safe distance away from the ledge.

He grinned at her. "Are you afraid of heights?"

"No." She peered at the cold, hard ground twenty-odd feet below her and laughed. "I'm afraid of falling." She eyed him with curiosity. "You aren't though, are you?"

"Nope." He scooted back about a foot until he was even with her, then crossed his legs. "My dad is really into rock climbing, and he started teaching my sisters and me when we were barely able to walk. One of my earliest memories is him holding me against a short climbing wall to practice finding handholds. My arms were too short to do much, but I loved the idea of climbing high above the ground."

"Wow." She shook her head. "I don't think you ever told me before that you were into rock climbing. I've never been." Her eyes darted back to the barn's floor and she shivered. "Although, I'm not so sure I ever want to."

"Oh, I bet you'd love it," Taylor said. "When you're up there on top of a huge rock and can see for miles around, it's all worth it." He opened the box of pastries from the Sea Star Bakery and selected one.

Meg unscrewed the lid of the metal Thermos and poured its contents into the two mugs, pushing one across the floor to him. He still hadn't said anything about what he thought of the barn. She wanted to ask, but was almost afraid to hear his response. She grabbed a cinnamon twist from the box he'd brought and bit into it, showering her lap with crystals of spiced sugar. She eyed her pants with dismay. Although she'd worn her oldest pair of denim jeans to work in the barn, she hadn't expected for them to get dirty quite so soon.

Taylor laughed. "I think you're wearing more of that donut than you've eaten."

Her cheeks burned and she brushed the sugar off onto the dusty wooden planks of the loft. What was a little more debris added to what had already accumulated over fifty years of neglect?

"I'm sorry, I didn't mean to offend you." He popped the rest of his bearclaw into his mouth and wiped his hands on his jeans. "You're usually so buttoned up."

She pulled her head back. "Buttoned up?"

"Yeah, you know, like in control of the situation." He shook his head. "You're always so cool and collected in the kitchen, no matter what happens. And you seem so sure of what you want out of life."

She stared at him. He thought she had things together? Although she was in her element in the kitchen, she still sometimes felt like she was running around like a chicken with her head cut off. "I wouldn't say I have my life together," she murmured under her breath.

He cocked his head to the side. "What did you say? I didn't catch that."

She flashed him a smile, then took a swig of coffee before standing. "Nothing. Just something silly." She gestured to all of the garbage in the barn. "So, what do you think?"

Her stomach twisted as he stood slowly and put his hands on his hips, looking around again. His expression gave no indication of what he was thinking, and he took his time before speaking.

"I like it." He smiled widely at her. "I can see a lot of potential here."

She let out her breath in an audible whoosh.

He looked at her with concern. "Are you okay? Is the hay bothering you? We should probably open all of the doors and windows while we're working because we're going to disturb a lot of dust."

She grinned like a fool, her heart filling with happiness. Taylor was an accomplished chef and restaurant manager. If he thought the barn had potential, her crazy dream might not be so impossible after all. "Actually, I'm great. Can I tell you what I'm thinking for organizing the space? Once we get everything cleared out of here, of course."

"I'd love to hear about it." He tapped his chin with his finger as he regarded the space. "Actually, I was thinking the loft would make a great dining area. Imagine what it would look like with tables along a railing here and then a special table under the window."

"That's exactly what I was thinking!" Meg wanted to wrap her arms around him. After Theo's lack of excitement, it felt good to share her vision with someone who understood. "If everything works out, I'm planning to put the kitchen under the loft, and then open up most of the main room for seating, although I may have a few other rooms along the sides for private dining. It'll work well for larger banquets or for smaller parties." Her ideal restaurant shimmered like a thin veil over the barn's current condition as she glimpsed into the future.

Taylor sneezed loudly, snapping her back to the present.

"Gesundheit." She grinned at him. "Maybe it's time to open up those doors now and let a little fresh air in here."

They packed up their breakfast and brought it back down to the main floor, setting it on an old bureau by the door. She removed two dust masks and two pairs of leather gloves from her bag and handed one of each to Taylor.

"So where should we start?" he asked, his eyes darting around to take in the massive space.

She had that odd feeling again that the walls of the barn were closing in on her. After taking a deep breath, she focused on the task at hand. "I think we should try to do this in an orderly fashion. Let's designate locations where we can have piles for things to keep, throw, or donate."

He nodded, and they got to work, removing small items from on top of larger objects and placing them in the appropriate pile.

"Is this an old tractor?" Taylor lifted the corner of a tan canvas tarp off of an object hulking in the far corner and peeked under it.

"Yep. Shawn mentioned there was one in here. I think

he's going to try to fix it up for them to use." The green paint on the old John Deere had chipped in places and the rubber tires had long ago deflated and started to disintegrate onto the cement floor of the barn, but the metal frame appeared solid. "I don't think we're going to get that thing out of here by ourselves, so we should try to make an access path for Shawn. Once it's gone, there will be a lot more room in here."

Taylor walked past the tractor. "I'm guessing we're tossing these mattresses?"

She took one look at the soiled, mildewy twin mattresses leaning against the wall and recoiled. "Yeah. Those are definitely trash." They each grabbed a mattress with gloved hands and dragged them out in front of the barn. Shawn had ordered a large dumpster from the local refuse company, but it wasn't scheduled to arrive until later in the day.

They moved a kayak to one side of the barn to evaluate for seaworthiness, then added a set of brass light fixtures to the keep pile. "Zoe might like some of these for the guest rooms in the Inn." Meg rubbed away a patch of dust from one of the frosted light shades to appraise their condition. No visible cracks. She set it down with care. "I saw something similar to these in one of the antique shops on Main Street."

Taylor stopped what he was doing and nodded approvingly. "I bet there's a lot of old furnishings in here that would be nice for the Inn. George Camden may have his faults, but I admire how much thought he put into the decor of the Willa Bay Lodge. He managed to keep a historical feel for much of it, while still making it modern enough for current-day guests."

"Me too. I always loved walking the halls of the Lodge. It was like taking a step back into history." She closed her eyes briefly, envisioning the bare interior of the Inn at Willa Bay. They'd had some issues getting the roof replaced, so Zoe was behind on getting the rooms renovated. "I think Zoe plans to do the same with the Inn. I know she's really curious about the resort's past."

"What about this?" Taylor rested a gloved hand on the scratched top of a chest of drawers hiding behind a few round tables leaning up against it. "This might be nice to have in one of the rooms."

Meg narrowed her eyes at it. "Hmm. I don't know. It's pretty beat up, but I bet it's solid wood. I'll have to ask Zoe what she thinks about refurbishing it. Let's leave it and the tables here for now."

They continued moving things out of the barn into piles until late afternoon, only pausing for a quick lunch. When the dumpster finally arrived, they threw away what couldn't be salvaged, leaving behind a much smaller pile of furniture and other odds and ends they'd dragged out that day that could potentially be used at the Inn.

Taylor stood back, wiping the sweat from his brow with the back of his hand. "I don't think I've worked this hard in a long time."

"Me neither." Meg took a slug of water from the bottle she'd refilled at the Inn when they'd eaten lunch. She'd cancelled her gym membership soon after the purchase of the resort and hadn't regretted her decision for a moment. There was more than enough physical work to be done on the property, so she had no need for scheduled exercise.

Taylor walked back into the barn, and she followed. What she saw was disheartening. Although they'd half-filled the dumpster and removed a bunch of furniture, they'd barely made a dent.

"This is going to take a while," Taylor observed.

"No kidding." She bit her lip, hoping she wouldn't

start crying. After the long day of physical exertion, her emotions were close to the surface. With both of them working all day, they'd only gotten through about ten percent of the junk. How was she going to get the rest of it done by October?

"Hey," he said, patting her on the shoulder. "It's going to be okay."

He'd spent one of his few days off helping her clean out an old barn that he had no stake in. That was a true friend. His kindness overwhelmed her, and tears slipped down her cheeks. He rubbed her back to comfort her. All she wanted to do was to collapse into his arms, but she couldn't. While he may no longer be her boss, he wasn't her boyfriend either.

She wiped her eyes with the cleanest part of her sleeve she could find and unsuccessfully attempted to smile. "Thanks. I'm just a little overwhelmed by how much there is to do."

He pressed his lips together, gazed up at the rafters, and sighed, then returned his attention to her. "If you'd like, I can come out here to help you again next week."

"I couldn't ask you to do that," she mumbled, trying to keep her emotions at bay. "I'm sure you have a million other things to do."

He took another look around the barn, sighed again, and ran a hand over his jet-black hair as he gave her a small smile. "There's nothing I'd rather do than help a friend in need."

"Thanks." Although she'd detected hesitation in his offer, she wasn't in a position to turn him down. Getting the barn ready for renovations by October was a long shot at this point, but it was all she had to hang onto, and she needed all of the help she could get.

6

Tia

"Hey." Tia moved a chair directly in front of a young bride sitting sideways on the couch in the living room of the Inn, carefully avoiding the skirt of her puffy white bridal gown, which took up most of the couch and spilled out over the floor. "What's going on?"

Another woman, wearing a long, strapless purple bridesmaid's dress, paced over to the window, then back to the couch. She sighed loudly. "I think she's got cold feet about marrying Derek."

That was fairly evident. Although she was dabbing at her eyes with a soggy Kleenex, the bride's face resembled a raccoon's. Jet-black mascara formed blurred rivulets as it streaked down her pink cheeks. The rims of her eyes were red from crying and errant strands of golden hair had plastered themselves to her wet skin.

The mother-of-the-bride stood behind the couch, frantically attempting to fix her daughter's ornately arranged updo. "Melinda, you've got to stop crying. Your makeup is running and your hair's a mess."

Melinda didn't appear to hear her. If she did, her mother's admonition hadn't helped, because a new surge of tears and loud weeping followed. "What if I'm making a big mistake?" she wailed. "What if Derek isn't The One?"

"Oh, honey," her mother said. "I'm sure you're not making a mistake. You love Derek." She gave up on fixing her daughter's hair, came around the sofa to sit next to her, and squeezed her hand.

"But..." Melinda's words dissolved into another fit of blubbering.

The pacing bridesmaid sighed again, and Melinda's mother glared at her. "Missy, your sister is upset, and your attitude isn't helping."

Tia had been coordinating weddings for years, and this wasn't anything she hadn't seen before. She turned to Melinda's mother and sister. "Could I have a moment alone with her?"

The older woman looked at her with skepticism, then threw her hands up in the air. "I suppose it couldn't hurt. I can't seem to talk any sense into her." She peered at the clock on the wall. "Is that clock right? Is it already four?"

Tia nodded.

"The wedding's supposed to start now." Melinda's mother's face paled. "All those people are out there, waiting for her to walk down the aisle. Derek is waiting for her."

Melinda gave a loud sob and buried her face in her shredded tissue.

Tia looked in the direction of the lawn in front of the gazebo, where the ceremony would take place. The long brocade curtains in the living room were closed tightly to provide privacy to the bride as she got ready, but Tia knew the mother was right. The guests would already be seated, and as soon as Tia gave the cue, the staff would play the Wedding March. Still, they had time before anyone knew something was wrong.

"It will be fine. Let's get the two of you out to the porch so you can join up with everyone else to prepare for the ceremony. I'll let you know as soon as it's time to begin." Tia firmly nudged the older woman out of the room. The bridesmaid followed them outside to where the rest of the wedding party was gathered.

When she returned to the living room, Tia pushed the door closed and walked slowly back to the couch. Although she was confident she could turn the situation around, it didn't stop her pulse from thundering in her ears. She hadn't worked at the Inn at Willa Bay for very long and having a runaway bride wouldn't look good on her track record.

However, she didn't think that would be an issue with this bride and groom. She'd met with both Melinda and Derek several times during the wedding planning process and had rarely seen two people who were more in love. She saw a lot of engaged couples, and although she didn't know the fates of their marriages after they left the reception, she had her suspicions about some of them.

Melinda and her fiancé were different. Derek seemed genuinely sweet with her—always happy to run back to the car to get his fiancée a jacket if she was cold, or give input on the wedding with a willingness to compromise. Yes, Melinda had found herself a good man. Tia herself would be thrilled to have someone like Derek in her life.

Melinda sniffled as Tia approached her. "Do you think I'm being silly?" she asked.

"No, I don't think you're being silly." Tia pulled the armchair closer to the couch, gently pushing the delicate material of her skirt out of the way. "Marriage is a big commitment."

Melinda nodded. "I know. And I thought I was ready, but..."

"But it's scary."

Melinda nodded again.

"Do you love Derek?" Tia leaned forward and locked eyes with the woman. "Do you want to marry him?"

Melinda's eyes lit up through the mist of tears. "I do," she whispered. "He's everything I ever wanted."

"Okay, then." Tia smiled at her. "It's perfectly normal to have some doubts, but I think you're ready for this." She reached behind her to grab a clean tissue and handed it to Melinda.

Melinda gave her a weak smile.

"Let's try taking a few deep breaths." Tia inhaled to the count of five, then slowly exhaled, watching to make sure Melinda followed suit.

After a few rounds of focused breathing, Melinda closed her eyes and relaxed into the sofa for a moment. When she opened them, she said, "So what do I do now? According to my mom, I've wrecked my hair and makeup. I don't have time to go back to the salon and get them fixed."

Tia sprang to her feet. "Don't worry about it. I've got you covered. Follow me." She led the bride over to a small white vanity tucked against the wall and pulled out the swivel chair for her.

"Oh no," Melinda's eyes widened as she caught a glimpse of her reflection in the long oval mirror. "I look horrible."

Tia smiled at her reassuringly. "Only temporarily." She had Melinda turn away from the mirror, then opened a drawer in the vanity and retrieved her emergency-cosmetics kit, a comb with a spiked handle, a can of extra-strength hairspray, and a variety of hairpins. She'd always been good with hair and makeup and had briefly considered a career in cosmetology before deciding on being an event planner. She quickly assessed the damage, then got to work. Once Melinda's face was clean, Tia pinned any wayward hairs back into place, gave the ornate updo a quick coating of hairspray, and fixed the bride's makeup.

When she was finished, she spun her back around to face the mirror. This time, Melinda beamed at her image. "I don't know how you did it, but I look even better than I did after leaving the beauty salon." She lightly touched her hair. "I love it."

Tia helped her to a standing position, then stepped back. "You look gorgeous."

Melinda's lips quivered and Tia held up her hand. "Now don't start crying again. I'm running out of mascara!"

They both laughed, and Melinda's cheeks took on a natural blush that made her glow.

"Are you ready?" Tia asked.

"I am." Melinda leaned forward and wrapped her arms around Tia. "Thank you so much. I don't know what I would have done without you."

"You're very welcome." A wave of emotion came over Tia. Being a wedding coordinator wasn't always a glamorous job, but it had its perks. She loved being a part of one of the most important days in someone's life, even if she'd only known them for a short time.

Melinda stayed hidden in the entry hall while Tia went outside to inform the wedding party the ceremony was about to begin.

"Is she okay?" Melinda's mother asked, worry ringing in her voice.

Tia patted her on the arm. "She's great. All ready to go."

"Thank you." The deep creases lining her face smoothed out considerably as she relaxed. She gave Tia a side hug. "I appreciate your help."

"Of course. That's what I'm here for." Tia smiled at her, then signaled for the music to start. "Okay, everyone. It's showtime."

The ushers led the mothers of the bride and groom to their seats, followed soon after by the bridesmaids and groomsmen. When it was time for Melinda to walk down the aisle, Tia slipped out behind her and stood in an unobtrusive spot near the back of the seating area.

Derek's face held a mixture of terror and utter happiness as he waited on the steps of the gazebo. As his gaze fell on his bride, any trace of concern disappeared, and a humongous grin lit up his face. He and Melinda locked eyes and she walked toward him with a bounce in her step, her smile just as wide as his. Tia grinned too. Yes, they were going to make it.

The scent of the roses climbing the white latticework of the newly rebuilt gazebo wafted through the air. Behind it, the sun shimmered on the calm blue waters of Willa Bay and gulls flew high overhead, creating the perfect atmosphere for an outdoor wedding.

Tia watched from afar as the couple tied the knot. When they were back down the aisle, she gave them a few minutes alone, then guided the newlyweds and their wedding party over to the side of the Inn to form a receiving line.

While some of the guests exchanged pleasantries with the bride and groom, other attendees milled around, drinking wine and beer from the open bar. Everything looked good there, so Tia made her way through the crowds to check on the dinner preparations.

Debbie and Libby's catering company, Willa Bay Provisions, had been hired for the event. Tia found them working in the Inn's kitchen, laying out the prepared food that they'd brought ready to serve. She breathed in the mouthwatering scent of beef medallions in mushroom sauce and garlic mashed potatoes. The bride and groom had asked for something simple but delicious, and if the smells coming from the kitchen were any indication, they were going to be very happy with what they'd ordered for their reception. The caterers looked like they had everything under control and Tia didn't want to bother them, so she left quickly.

The outdoor dining area, though, was a different story. The tables had been set as ordered with white linens and purple napkins in silver napkin holders, but Zoe was talking with the setup staff—and she didn't look pleased.

Tia hurried over. "Is there something wrong?"

Zoe's eyes darted across the rows of tables, then down to the iPad she always had with her. She tapped on the screen. "We need a few more tables. There are fourteen more guests than we'd expected."

"Fourteen over the extra ten that Melinda told us about?"

Zoe nodded and Tia's blood ran cold. All the tables the rental company had dropped off earlier had been set up, and there were no extras. At this time of day, it would be difficult to rent more. Her mind raced, and a vision of the barn surfaced in her thoughts.

"I think I saw some round tables in the barn."

Zoe looked up. "Really? I didn't think there was anything usable in there."

"I can't make any promises, but I'll check them out. Do Debbie and Libby know about the additional guests?"

"They said there's plenty of food, and we have extra linens and table settings. If you can find at least two decent-sized tables, we should be golden." Zoe swiped her finger over the iPad and marked off a box, then tucked it under her arm. "I have to go check on some other things, but let me know if you find some tables." Her lips twisted into a grimace. "The guests who didn't RSVP may end up eating on the porch." Tia had to admit that solution was tempting, but they both knew it wouldn't look good for their new event venue to already be running into problems, even if it wasn't their fault.

"I'll go right now." Tia speed-walked toward the barn, slowing as she passed the crowds of wedding guests. She flashed her best smile at them. Once she was out of sight, she broke into a jog.

When she arrived, she eyed the large dumpster in the clearing next to the barn. Meg and her friend Taylor had been working on the cleanout earlier in the week, and with any luck, they hadn't thrown out the tables she was picturing. Tia flung open the door and peered inside. Her eyes took a minute to adjust to the dim light, but when they did, she breathed a sigh of relief.

The three round tables she'd remembered were still there, leaning against an old chest of drawers that had seen better days. Dust puffed into the air as her feet pounded across the cement floor. She maneuvered one of the heavy wooden tables away from the others to get a good look at it. It was covered in cobwebs and a thick layer of grime—but it seemed structurally sound, and that was all she cared about. As long as they were safe enough for the guests, a good cleaning and a long tablecloth could hide a myriad of flaws.

She set it against the wall and went to check out the next one—which had a bent leg that stuck out like it was trying to trip someone. Not even a pretty tablecloth could fix that abnormality. She crossed her fingers, then pulled out the third table. Thank goodness—it was fine. She leaned it against the other good one. She would have liked to take one with her, but they were too bulky to move on her own.

Before leaving, she took a long look around. She didn't have much reason to spend time on this part of the resort grounds. It was only by chance that Shawn had shown her the interior of the barn on a tour of the property when she'd first been hired.

The barn meant a lot to Meg, but Tia couldn't see how there was any chance this structure could ever become a restaurant. There was so much junk in here that clearing everything out was going to take several months, not to mention all of the structural repair work that would be needed before any interior remodeling could happen.

Poor Meg. Tia's schedule was packed with all the weddings they'd booked recently, but she'd become friendly with Meg over the last two months working at the Inn, and wished there was something she could do to help her out. For now, though, she needed to focus on solving the immediate problem.

Tia returned to the event and sent a few staff members to retrieve the tables from the barn. Everything was set up just in time for the guests to trickle in and find their seats.

Zoe and Tia hung back, watching as the maid of honor toasted her best friend, and the best man roasted the groom. The bride and groom took it all in good humor, laughing along with their guests.

Zoe motioned to the head table. "You did a great job on this wedding. Look how happy they are."

Her praise warmed Tia's heart. "Thanks. I think it turned out pretty good." She laughed under her breath. "Even the fiasco with the extra guests."

Zoe shrugged. "That kind of stuff always happens. You just have to take it in stride." She turned away from the reception to fully face Tia. "I was really impressed with how you handled the bride before the ceremony. Her mother made a point to tell me how well you did calming her down."

Tia's cheeks burned. "Thank you. I had a feeling that it was just a case of pre-wedding jitters. She and Derek are a good couple."

Zoe nodded and eyed her appraisingly. "Knowing how to recognize that quality is a skill that can't be taught, but it's something a good wedding coordinator needs to have." She wrapped her arms around Tia for a quick hug.

Tia was taken aback by the gesture from her boss. Zoe frequently demonstrated affection toward her friends and family, but until now she'd always kept Tia at a professional distance. "Thanks Zoe. Your support means a lot to me. I haven't found that everywhere."

Zoe raised an eyebrow and looked like she was about to say something, but Tia's phone vibrated loudly in the small purse she wore during events. Tia hastily pulled it out and silenced it, checking the caller ID. She looked up at Zoe. "Is it okay if I take this?"

"Sure. I'll stay here and make sure no new problems crop up. Take a break. You've been working hard tonight." Zoe smiled at her and turned her attention back to the reception.

Moving away from the boisterous crowd, Tia pressed the phone to her ear. "Hello?"

"Well, you finally answered," her mother said. Tia winced. Marta Ortiz wasn't known for mincing words.

"Is everything okay? Is Abuela doing all right?" The only reason Tia decided to answer the phone call from her mother was because her grandmother had recently been ill. As much as she didn't want to talk to her mom, she'd never forgive herself if she ignored a call about her grandmother.

"Abuela's fine." Tia's mother sighed dramatically. "That woman is going to outlive us all." There was no love lost between Marta and her mother-in-law. "Her cardiologist said the medication she's on now is controlling her heart condition very well."

Tia let out her breath. "Okay, good." She steeled herself before asking, "So why are you calling?"

"Can't a mother call her own daughter?" Marta's voice held more than a tinge of indignation.

"Yes, Mom. Of course you can call me. So, what's going on?" Tia walked away from the Inn, toward the row of cottages where both Shawn and Zoe lived.

"I wanted to share with you some good news. Angela is engaged!"

"Oh." Tia focused on the rhythmic sound of her feet crunching on gravel. Angela, Tia's younger sister, had been dating her boyfriend, Robert, for several years now, so this announcement wasn't exactly a shock. "That's great. When are they getting married?"

Her mother's words bubbled out almost before Tia finished her question. "Sometime next summer. We're all so excited for them. It's about time one of you girls settled down."

Tia took a few deep breaths. Marta's point was obvious. She wasn't shy about her desire to see all four of her girls married off. Tia's older brother, Antonio, was free to live his life doing who knew what, but there were expectations for the girls in the family.

The cottages were in sight now, their cheerful paint colors calming her. Zoe's had been painted a bright turquoise, whereas Shawn had done his in the same mellow orange she'd seen in the sunsets over the bay. From what Tia had heard, Zoe had been living on the property for over a decade, and after doing some renovations, Shawn had recently moved into the cottage next to hers. The rest of the cottages perched along the cliff overlooking the bay were empty and rundown from years of neglect—something Shawn hoped to remedy soon.

Her mother's voice cut through her thoughts. "Tia? Are you still there?"

"I'm still here. Mom, I'm actually working right now."

"It's seven o'clock at night there."

"It's a Saturday, and I'm a wedding coordinator. I'll be here until close to midnight." Tia waited for her mother's response, and Marta delivered as expected.

"It's just a wedding. I don't understand why people even need a coordinator. My mother and aunt helped me with everything for mine."

"Well, not everyone has a mother or aunt to help. They need someone like me to make sure everything goes according to plan." Tia's patience was wearing thin. Her mother had never understood her desire to be a wedding planner. When Tia had decided to get a degree in event planning from the local community college instead of going to a four-year university, Marta didn't speak to her for over a week.

Of course, Tia's brother and all of her sisters had gone to college, just like their parents wanted. Two of her sisters were enrolled in medical school and her brother did something in finance. None of them could understand why someone as smart as Tia would want to become a wedding planner.

Their lack of understanding was a big reason why Tia had moved halfway across the country, from West Texas to Willa Bay. She'd heard about the small town known as "The Wedding Capital of the Northwest" while working at an event-planning firm in her hometown of El Paso. It had seemed like the perfect place to make a new life for herself, far away from her family's meddling and opinions.

"Fine. I'll let you go," Marta huffed. "But we need to have a heart-to-heart talk sometime soon. You've never been the responsible type, and your father and I don't like you living so far away from us."

Her mother's implications were clear: she didn't think Tia could handle being on her own. There may have been a time when that was true—when she'd been fresh out of high school and naïve about a lot of things in the world. But the credit card debt she'd racked up from splurges at the mall and partying with her friends were a thing of the past. She'd worked her fingers to the bone to pay off her debt, and now lived a very minimalist lifestyle—not that her parents would ever admit how far she'd come.

"I'm twenty-six," Tia said, "and I like living here. Anyway, I have to go. I think someone's trying to get my attention." She hated lying, but she needed to extricate herself from this conversation before her mother's digs at her career and life choices made headway into her psyche. "I'll talk to you later. Give my love to everyone." She hung up the phone, just as her mother started to say something else.

Zoe had told her to take a fifteen-minute break, and she still had about half of that left, so she continued on down the lane. She passed by the first nineteen cottages, then stopped in front of the last one, her favorite.

Once upon a time, it had been painted a shade of pink, but now only specks of the original color remained. Since the first time Tia laid eyes on the small porch, charming front window, and glimpse of the water through the overgrown brush on the opposite side of the road, it had enchanted her.

She sat on the porch steps to take in her surroundings. Being this far away from the main event grounds gave the impression that she wasn't even on the resort property anymore. Only two of the other cottages were visible from this vantage point, and the noise from the wedding was barely audible. Here, it was just her, the birds twittering in the bushes, and the squirrels racing around the trees. This was the space to mature that she'd been hoping for in her move to Willa Bay.

After a few minutes, she reluctantly stood and walked back toward the wedding. Zoe probably wouldn't mind if she took an extended break, but being new, Tia wanted to put her best foot forward. She couldn't allow the issues with her family to affect her work. This was *her* event to manage, and she intended to make sure it was the best wedding any of the guests had ever attended.

7

Sam knocked on the front door of her parents' house. She'd grown up here, and it still felt odd to not use her own key. She waited on the porch, holding a bag of potato chips – her contribution to the family BBQ. The sound of footsteps approaching was almost masked by the cacophony of screaming children. She then heard her mother's voice shouting just beyond the door, "Knock it off! You're going to need to go outside if you can't keep it down."

Sam bit back a smile. Briggs family dinners were never quiet affairs, especially with Libby's four kids in attendance. However, her mom seemed more on edge tonight than usual, if she was bothering to say anything about the noise.

Debbie flung the door open, and her face immediately erupted in a huge grin. "Sam! I'm so happy to see you!" She wrapped her arms around her daughter so tightly that Samantha had to adjust her body to catch her breath.

"Hey, Mom." Samantha rested her head on Debbie's shoulder, like she had so many times before. Her fingers pressed into her mother's back, savoring the emotional and physical warmth of the loving embrace. When Debbie eased her grip, Sam stepped back, inhaling the comforting floral scent of her mother's favorite perfume.

Debbie didn't let go of Sam completely, holding her at arm's length to get a good look at her. "You got sunburnt."

Sam laughed. "Yeah, that tends to happen in the Caribbean. I swear I put on a ton of sunscreen every day."

"But you look happy too." Debbie cocked her head to the side. "Less stressed than the last time I saw you."

"Probably because I just got back from two weeks on a cruise ship." Sam smiled at her. Working on the boat hadn't been a vacation in the normal sense of the word, but it had been a nice reprieve from everything back home. She'd only been back in Willa Bay for two days and the reality of her real life was already crashing down on her.

"I bet Brant was happy to see you," Debbie said. "He probably missed you a lot while you were gone." She eyed Sam expectantly.

"Uh-huh. He did." Sam hadn't seen Brant since they'd broken up weeks before. A sharp pang of guilt stole her breath for a moment. Although she didn't want to be romantically involved with Brant anymore, he'd been her best friend and she mourned the loss of his friendship.

"Is he working tonight?" Her mom looked past her, as though hoping to see Brant lurking by the car. "I was hoping he'd come to dinner. We haven't seen him in a while either."

"No, sorry. He wasn't able to make it." Sam hated the sadness on her mother's face. Telling her about the breakup wouldn't be easy, and she intended to put it off for as long as possible. She didn't want to deal with all of her family's opinions on the subject when she was still trying to work through her own feelings.

Debbie nodded. "That's too bad. Well, come in. Everyone will be excited to see you." She stepped aside to allow Sam room to enter the house.

A little girl zoomed across their path as they walked toward the kitchen, moving so fast that Sam couldn't tell by the flash of golden hair which of Libby's two daughters it had been. In the living room, a young boy, most likely Sam's nephew, Tommy, shouted angrily at one of his siblings about stealing a toy.

Debbie grimaced and rubbed her temples. "They're louder than usual. I'm not sure how much more of this I can take."

They entered the kitchen, which was connected to both a small family room on one side and a formal dining room on the other. Libby rushed around the kitchen, grabbing burger fixings from the refrigerator and setting them on the counter. Debbie took plates down from an upper cupboard and carried them out to the dining room.

"Hey, Sam." Libby, still gripping a package of American cheese in one hand, strode around the kitchen island and wrapped an arm around her sister.

"Hey, Libby." Sam hugged her back, then raised an eyebrow. "You've got enough food here for several small armies."

Libby laughed. "That's about what our family is getting to be. You have no idea how much four growing children eat, especially the boys." She rolled her eyes. "Some days, William eats more food than Gabe and I combined."

Sam nodded. "I can imagine." She couldn't picture having four kids though. When she'd been with Brant, they'd talked about having one child, maybe two at the most. The idea of four was overwhelming.

"Okay, I can't deal with this noise anymore," Debbie said as she walked back into the kitchen. "Libby, can you send them outside, please?"

Libby studied their mom's face, then nodded. "Sure. Of course." She went into the hallway and yelled at top volume. "Kids! All of you outside! Now!"

"Me too?" William, Libby's oldest child asked from his seat on the family room couch where he'd been playing on his tablet.

"Yeah. You too. Hand over the tablet and go play outside with Dad and Grandpa." Libby held out her hand and William reluctantly released his electronic device. The kids filed outside, and Libby slid the glass door closed. "That ought to keep them busy for a while. Gabe and Dad can deal with them."

Debbie frowned. "Sorry. Usually I love having them around, but I have a bit of a headache today."

"No problem," Libby said breezily. "They were driving me nuts too." She surveyed the kitchen. "Okay. I need someone to slice the tomatoes and onions, someone to wash the lettuce, and someone to set the table."

"I'll do the lettuce," Sam said.

"No. I'll do that," Libby said. "I already have the colander out. How about you set the table instead."

"Sure." Sam wasn't sure why her older sister had even given them an option if she already had plans for what each person should do, but it wasn't worth it to argue with her. Sam got the silverware out, then started setting the table with the plates her mother had already brought out.

Libby came up beside her and switched the knife from the left of the plate to the right. "You put them on the wrong side."

Sam eyed her sister. "Really? Does it matter? This isn't a catering event."

Libby stuck her hands on her hips. "It matters." She pivoted and returned to the kitchen.

Sam took a satisfying moment to glare at Libby's back, then reluctantly swapped the placement of the silverware she'd already laid out. Being the baby of the family, sometimes her sisters and parents still treated her like a little kid.

"Okay, I'm done," she announced. "Is there anything else that you trust me to help with?" Her tone was snarky, but she didn't really care.

Debbie looked up from the stack of onions she was slicing. "I'm about done here. Let me get these on a platter and then I need to get some things out of the refrigerator in the garage. Would you mind helping me with that?"

"Sure." Sam walked over to the sliding glass door and peered into the backyard. The kids had settled down and the three oldest were tossing a football with Libby's husband while Kaya and her grandfather threw a softball back and forth.

"Okay, I'm ready," Debbie announced from behind Sam. They walked out to the garage together and Debbie opened the refrigerator, which was packed with hamburger buns, jars of pickles, and several bottles of ketchup, mustard, and mayonnaise. Debbie looked at Sam sheepishly and handed her three plastic bags full of hamburger buns. "There was a sale at the grocery store, so I stocked up a bit. You never know how much people will eat at these dinners."

Sam laughed. "Or you just can't resist a good sale." Her mom was well known for her bargain shopping.

Debbie's face darkened. "I don't get much time for grocery shopping anymore. Or, for that matter, much of anything besides the business." She ducked her head into the refrigerator and rooted around for something in the back.

When Debbie found what she was looking for and emerged from the fridge again, Sam asked, "Is that what's been bothering you? You seem a little, um, upset."

Debbie put bottles and jars of condiments on top of the big chest freezer next to the fridge, then leaned against it and stared at the floor. When she looked up, tears shimmered in her eyes. "I'm a little overwhelmed with the catering business. I'd just gotten used to having time for myself before we bid on all of these new jobs. Libby wants us to expand the business and I don't want to let her down, but I can't even enjoy having the kids around when they're here because I'm so on edge about everything."

Sam set the hamburger buns down on the freezer and hugged her mom. "I'm sure she doesn't want you to be unhappy though. Can you tell her you don't want to take on so many events?"

Debbie shook her head. "No. She needs the work."

Sam wasn't sure what Debbie was referring to, but this didn't seem like the time to pry into Libby's life. "What if I helped with the business again? I have some time before school starts." School was scheduled to start in two weeks, and there was very little chance of her getting another job as a PE teacher before then, but she was still holding on to that small bit of hope. "Maybe you could spend some time out of the house doing things for you. Didn't you have that group of friends that knitted hats for chemo patients?"

Debbie nodded. "Yeah. But I haven't met with them in months. I meant to go last month, but something came up."

"I think you should do it," Sam said. "You need to

take some time for yourself." That was one of the things that had become evident on the cruise ship. Being away from everyone she knew had given her a lot of time to think.

The stairs on the exterior of the garage, coming down from Meg's apartment above, creaked loudly and the side door opened.

"Sam!" Meg ran over to her, gave her a hug, then slugged her lightly in the arm. "You had all of us worried. I can't believe you were having fun on a Caribbean cruise this whole time."

"Well, it wasn't exactly a vacation, but yeah." Sam grinned at her. "I had a good time."

While Meg was distracted, Debbie turned away from them and ran her hand over her eyes. Although their conversation had been interrupted, Sam hoped her mother had taken her advice to heart. She was obviously hurting, and it would do her good to do something for herself for once.

Meg glanced at the food stacked on the freezer. "Do you need any help carrying this in?"

Debbie smiled at her, seemingly recovered. "Unless we want a jar of pickles dropped on the floor, we could definitely use some help."

Meg shuddered. "Yeah, no. My whole apartment upstairs would stink of brine." She carefully scooped up a jar of pickles and a bag of bread. Debbie and Sam grabbed the remaining items and they carried it all into the house.

Libby had everything arranged on the table when they arrived. "The burgers will be done in about ten minutes." She narrowed her eyes at Samantha. "Which gives me just enough time to grill you about going off the grid these last few weeks."

Sam squirmed under her big sister's scrutiny. "I wasn't off the grid. Brant knew where I was."

"Yeah, but he wouldn't tell us." Meg took an olive off the crudités platter and popped it into her mouth. "It was like he was avoiding everyone in the family."

A pit formed in Sam's stomach. It was probably because he was avoiding all of them. Her decision to dissolve their engagement had been a shock to him, and although he understood her reasons, he hadn't been happy about it.

"I'm sure he wasn't avoiding you guys." Her gaze roamed over the room, hoping for an excuse to change the subject.

Unfortunately, her sisters and mom weren't going to give up that easily.

"So how are wedding plans going?" Libby asked, pushing a plate about an inch closer to the center of the table to bring it in line with the others. "I bet you really missed him while you were gone."

Sam stared at the errant plate. "They're going." *Straight out the window,* she thought.

"Have you decided on a location yet?" Debbie asked. "We just catered a wedding at the Inn at Willa Bay, and it was gorgeous. Meg and Zoe have done a wonderful job there."

Meg blushed. "Aw, thanks, Mom."

"So?" Libby pressed. "Do you have a date? I want to get it on the books before our catering calendar fills up."

They weren't going to let go of this. Maybe it was better to rip off the bandage before she had to tell them any more lies.

She took a deep breath and said quickly, "Brant and I broke up."

Her mother's face filled with shock. "What?"

"You broke up with him?" Meg whispered. "Why?"

Libby eyed Sam with disbelief. "But you were like the perfect couple."

Sam took a step back to process their reactions. Libby thought they were perfect? That was ironic, because her oldest sister was the one with the perfect life. After a moment, she shrugged. "We've grown apart over the last year, and it didn't feel right anymore."

"Did something happen?" Meg asked. "If he cheated on you, I'll kill him."

From the look on Meg's face, Sam didn't doubt it. She eked out a small smile. "No need for a lynch mob. Nothing happened." She bit her lip. "I'd been unhappy for a while and I realized that we're just better as friends."

She briefly shut her eyes. Brant was a great guy, but she wanted something more. Maybe the burning passion that the movies portrayed wasn't realistic, but she wanted to find that out on her own.

When she looked up at her family, they were still staring at her like she'd sprouted wings.

"That's it? You're just giving up on your relationship?" Libby asked.

"No, that's not it." Sam tapped her fingers on the tabletop. "Brant and I had several long discussions about it and we both came to the conclusion that we should just be friends. We didn't have that strong connection that you need for marriage." She met each of their gazes in turn. "It was a mutual decision."

"But..." Libby started to say.

"No." Sam held up her hand. "This isn't something you have a say in."

Debbie still appeared shell-shocked, but she wrapped an arm around Sam. "I'm so sorry, honey. That must have been a difficult decision to make."

Sam leaned into her. "It was." All of the emotions she'd been trying to repress since the breakup crashed over her, and she fought to stay in control.

Meg patted her on the arm. "I always liked Brant, but I'm sure you had your reasons to break up with him." She cleared her throat and looked pointedly at Libby. "I think Sam's had enough of the inquisition. Can you check on the burgers?"

Libby opened her mouth, but then clamped her lips shut and nodded before sliding open the door and disappearing into the backyard.

Sam gave Meg a grateful look. "Thanks."

Meg nodded. "No problem."

The door opened again and the kids and everyone else spilled into the dining room. While they were washing hands and getting settled, Sam excused herself and went out the front door to sit on the porch. The noises inside were muffled, but she was blissfully alone. She hadn't wanted to ruin their family dinner with her news, but at least it was done now. She didn't need to worry about keeping the breakup a secret. There was still the matter of the loss of her job, but that could wait.

A sudden urge to smile surprised her. Her family's reaction had been upsetting, but now she was free. She could finally close the chapter in that part of her life and move on. She breathed in the sweet scent of the jasmine bushes her parents had planted when they'd bought their house over thirty years ago. She was single and jobless, but for the first time in months, she was bursting with hope for the future.

8

"Are you sure you'll be okay without me?" Debbie looked around the commercial kitchen she rented for her catering company, Willa Bay Provisions. They were catering a small retirement party for a local business that evening.

Libby sighed. "Mom. We'll be fine. We've got this." She eyed Samantha. "Right?"

Sam flashed her mom a bright smile. "Go to your meeting. Everything is under control."

"Are you sure?" Debbie hated leaving them with all of the preparations. In the past, she'd always been there to manage things, but after Sam had implored her to take time for her own interests, she'd made a last-minute decision to attend her monthly knitting group. "Sam hasn't done this in a while."

Her youngest daughter stared her down. "We'll be fine. I may be a little rusty, but it's not like cooking is something you forget how to do. Besides, this is a relatively small party and you'll be back later to help with the actual event. Stop worrying so much."

"Okay." Debbie looked at her daughters. Their expressions were a mixture of amusement and irritation. She inhaled deeply through her nostrils and let the oxygen flood her brain, calming her doubts. They were both intelligent women and experienced cooks. They could handle this. "I'm going to go now."

"Love you, Mom," Sam sang out. "Have fun."

Libby patted her back. "Go and have a good time with your friends."

Debbie nodded. "Bye, girls." She held her head high and exited the kitchen, not allowing herself to look back. She'd started the catering business years ago and she held everything they did to a high standard. Giving up some of that control was difficult, but if she wanted a life outside of the business, it was a necessary evil.

She got into her car, checking first to make sure she had all of her knitting supplies before leaving. On the seat next to her, colorful strands of spun fiber spilled out of an open bag made out of woven strips of fabric. Knitting needles stabbed through the balls of yarn, anchoring them in place.

Before getting out of the car at the Everton Community Center, Debbie glanced at the clock on the dashboard. Her resolve wavered. It seemed frivolous to take this time for herself and not help her girls prepare for the event. The catering business was her responsibility and she should be there.

Sam's words echoed in her ears: *Take some time for yourself.*

Deep down, Debbie knew Sam was right. Plus, if she took time for herself this one time, maybe she wouldn't be so resentful about taking on all of the additional catering jobs that Libby had committed them to. It would be okay. Sam and Libby had everything under control. Besides, the group she belonged to only met once a month, and was composed of other cancer survivors, like herself. They didn't just spend their meetings chatting, but also making hats to donate to chemotherapy patients at the local hospital. So, this wasn't an entirely selfish thing she was going to do.

She got out of the car and went around to the passenger side to remove the massive bag of knitting supplies, making sure everything was tucked in so it wouldn't fall out during the short trip into the center. Although she wouldn't need all of these materials for the two hour-long meeting, there had been too many times where she'd regretted not bringing a certain color of yarn or size of needle. It was always better to be overprepared.

When she pushed open the door of their usual meeting room, all five of the women seated at the table looked up and waved at her.

Shelby Dawes jumped out of her chair to greet her. "Debbie! I'm so glad you came. We've missed you." She gave Debbie a huge hug that brought tears of happiness to Debbie's eyes. It had been months, and she hadn't realized how sad it made her to not see her friends more regularly.

"I've missed all of you too." Debbie took her seat around the rectangular table and tucked her knitting bag under her chair. "I can't believe how long it's been. How are all of you?" Their membership fluctuated as people went through different stages of life, but there were normally around seven to eight people in attendance every month.

"I'm doing great," said a woman in her thirties with short blonde hair. "My latest scan came back clean."

"I'm so happy for you." Debbie smiled warmly at her.

"It's so nerve-wracking to wait for the results of those." She'd had a clean scan last April after being done with chemotherapy for a year, and it had been a huge relief for her whole family.

"My son is getting married," said another woman. "They've been living together for so long, we all wondered if it would ever happen."

"Congratulations." Debbie meant it, but her friend's news caused her a pang of envy. She'd been looking forward to Samantha's wedding and welcoming Brant into their family. Now the possibility of more grandchildren was a far-off prospect.

Debbie pulled out her knitting project and they all gabbed about friends and family members, needles clicking rhythmically as they stitched new rows on their hats. By the end of the meeting, she felt refreshed. It had been wonderful to connect with old friends and make a few new ones in the process. But someone she'd hoped to see hadn't shown up.

"Hey, do you know if Diana will be here next month? Has she been coming to the meetings?" Debbie asked. She and Diana had been chemo buddies, undergoing treatments at the same time and commiserating about all of the side effects over strawberry milkshakes at their favorite diner.

The women exchanged troubled glances, and even before they said something, a sinking feeling came over her. Her fingers ceased moving mid-stitch.

"Debbie, I'm sorry," Shelby said softly. "I thought you knew. Diana died a little over a month ago."

Debbie's head spun, her thoughts like loose pieces of string that wouldn't wind together. "No, I didn't know." Her stomach tightened as she asked, "How did it happen?"

"Her cancer came back and there wasn't anything they could do about it." Shelby's eyes held a heavy sadness. "Her family had a small memorial service for her back in July."

"Oh. I wish I'd known." Debbie stared at the stainless-steel knitting needles in her lap. If she concentrated on the hat, she wouldn't have to think about Diana. She resumed knitting, focusing on the way the multicolored yarn wove together to form a thick, warm layer that would keep a cancer patient's head warm during the colder months.

After about ten more minutes, the other women put away their projects and said their goodbyes, but Debbie didn't move from her spot.

"Are you okay?" Shelby stood next to Debbie, her bag slung over her shoulder. "I'm really sorry about Diana. I know you were good friends. I should have called you about her memorial service, but I thought you already knew."

Debbie finally stopped knitting and looked up. "Thanks. I'm okay. Just a little shocked and sad. It hurts when we lose one of the group."

"I know." Shelby sighed. "I just keep reminding myself that I'm still alive and I need to take advantage of that while I still can." She brightened. "In fact, my husband and I have decided to take a sabbatical from work and go on a six-month tour of Europe. Neither of us have ever been. I'd love to visit some of the historical sites and see some castles—I love castles."

"That's a good idea," Debbie said. "My husband and I have talked about taking a trip to Italy for years, but nothing ever comes of it."

Shelby grabbed her hands and looked her in the eyes. "You should do it. You won't regret it."

"I'll think about it." Debbie smiled and leaned down to pick up her bag. She set it on the table and put her materials away.

"Don't just think about it," Shelby advised. "You only get one life."

"Okay." Debbie stood, and lifted her bag off the table before wrapping one arm around her friend's shoulders. "I will definitely consider it." She doubted Peter could get the time away from work to take a two-week trip, but it was worth asking him again.

They walked out to the parking lot together and chatted for a few minutes before they each got into their own cars. Debbie stashed her yarn bag on the passenger seat and put her key in the ignition, but didn't start driving. She looked back at the community center and was struck by a wave of grief. Tears streamed down her cheeks, blurring her vision. The last time she'd seen Diana, they'd been at a knitting club meeting. They'd talked about grabbing a milkshake together sometime, but they'd both had busy lives and they'd never made it happen. Now she regretted not making time for her dear friend.

She grabbed a Kleenex to wipe away her tears, then started the engine and drove back to the catering kitchen. Before getting out of her car, she checked her reflection in the rearview mirror. After her crying jag, her mascara needed a light touch up, but there wasn't much she could do about the puffiness of her eyes. She crossed her fingers that her daughters wouldn't notice. There was no sense in worrying them about her own health by telling them about Diana's death.

Libby and Samantha looked up from packing all of the food into travel containers when Debbie entered and surveyed the kitchen. All of the dirty dishes had been placed in the dish sink and the counters were spotless. "Looks good, girls."

Libby beamed. "Thanks. Everything went according to plan." She tapped her finger on a piece of paper bearing a long column of jet-black checkmarks. "How was your meeting?"

Debbie pasted on a fake smile. "It was great. So nice to see everyone."

"You're hiding something." Sam peered at her. "Mom, you've never been great at keeping secrets."

"I'm not," she protested. "I had a nice time seeing everyone." That much was true, even if it wasn't the whole truth.

Libby scrutinized her too. "No, Sam's right. You're not telling us something."

Debbie strode over to the dish sink without answering. Those dishes weren't going to wash themselves. She slid a pair of heavy rubber gloves over her hands and turned on the water.

Libby tapped her on the shoulder. "Mom."

Debbie stared at the liquid splashing into the sink. Steam rose from the stainless-steel basin as the hot water accumulated in it.

"Mom." Libby reached past her to turn the faucet off. "What's wrong?"

Debbie braced herself on the edge of the sink. "Diana died." Her throat constricted. Saying it out loud made it all too real, and grief washed over her once more.

"Your friend from chemo?" Libby asked.

Debbie nodded. Her face crumpled and she leaned against the sink, bawling as her heart broke all over again.

"Oh, Mom." Libby wrapped her arms around her. "I'm so sorry."

Debbie's gloved hands lay limply on the edge of the

sink as Samantha came over and embraced her from the other side. The three of them stood huddled together for over a minute. All Debbie could do was cry. She'd never cried in front of the girls before, but now she couldn't stop. It was like all of her fears and regrets were coming out at once.

Finally, she stirred, ungloving and swiping her hand across her face. The girls stepped back, but didn't leave her.

Libby stroked her mom's hair, brushing it out of her face. Debbie's eldest daughter had always been the motherly type. "Is there anything we can do for you? Maybe a glass of water?"

Debbie tried to swallow, but it was like she had a dish sponge caught in her throat. "Water would be nice." Libby looked over at Sam, who nodded and jetted off toward the cupboard where they kept glassware. Debbie plucked a paper towel from the roll hanging over the counter and scrubbed at her face. "I'm sorry about falling apart. You girls shouldn't have had to see that."

Samantha returned with a glass of water and handed it to her. "Really? We're adults now. There's nothing wrong with letting us see you sad."

"Sam's right," Libby said. "We're always here for you, just like you've always been for us."

"Thanks." Debbie still felt sheepish for allowing her emotions to get the best of her in front of the girls, but she appreciated their concern. She glanced at Libby's checklist. "Now, I think we've wasted enough time on this. What else do we need to do before this evening?"

Libby went over to the counter and ran her finger down the list, while Sam remained with Debbie near the sink. "Mom," Sam whispered, "I'm sorry I told you to go to your knitting club meeting."

Debbie's heart melted. "Oh, honey, that wouldn't have changed anything." Part of her wished that she hadn't gone too, but she would have heard about Diana eventually.

"I know, but I hate for you to be so unhappy." Concern lined Samantha's face and her mouth turned down, as though she were about to break out into tears as well.

This time, it was Debbie's turn to comfort her daughter. She put both arms around her youngest child and pulled her close, kissing her forehead. "I'll be okay. This kind of news just takes a while to process." She allowed herself to relax in the familiar action of comforting her child. All of her daughters had grown up to be wonderful women and she had a lot to be proud of.

But was there more she should want out of life? Should she convince Peter to take that trip to Italy like Shelby had recommended? Diana's death made her own mortality frighteningly apparent. Why was Debbie still alive and Diana wasn't?

9

Taylor

"Thanks for helping me again." Meg opened the barn doors. "I felt a little depressed after last time. We worked so hard all day and didn't seem to make much progress."

Taylor didn't want to admit it, but he'd had the same thoughts. Cleaning out the barn was going to take a serious chunk of time. "No problem. I know how important this is to you."

"It is." She paused in the doorway and studied him with a peculiar expression on her face.

He struggled to stay still under her scrutiny. "What? Do I have powdered sugar around my mouth?" This time, instead of having breakfast in the barn, they'd joined Zoe, Shawn, and Celia on the front porch of the Inn for donuts, eggs, and coffee.

She laughed and broke her intense gaze. "No. I was just thinking about how much I appreciate your help. Not everyone would give up their day off to help a friend move junk." Her face darkened for a brief second. "Anyway, I was thinking we should start with some of the bigger furniture this time. If we clear out the larger items, it'll seem like we've made more progress, and I could really use that mental boost." She set her bag down near the door and handed him a pair of gloves and a dust mask.

"Sounds like a plan." He hated seeing her defeated. The sight of her tears the last time he'd helped her had been heart-wrenching. She'd chosen a huge project to tackle, and although she wasn't one to back down from a challenge, something like this would be daunting for anyone. He walked to the back of the barn where he remembered seeing a lot of furniture. "Hey, weren't there more tables here?" A table with a broken leg had been moved to the side, but he was sure there had been a couple others on his previous visit.

"I think Tia took them for a wedding. They were desperate, so she went scavenging." Meg shrugged. "Fewer things for us to lug out of here."

He nodded and pointed at the chest of drawers they'd uncovered before. "What about this? Did you ask Zoe about it?"

She shook her head. "No. I forgot to ask her. I need to do that so we can figure out what we're tossing or keeping."

"Want to take it outside so we can see it better?" He lifted one end of it to estimate the weight. "It's heavy, but I think we can manage."

"Sure." She grabbed the other side, but before they could move it very far, the second drawer from the bottom slid out.

Taylor reached out to steady the drawer before it could hit the ground. He tried to jockey it back into place, but it wasn't working.

"Is it caught on something?" Meg knelt on the ground

to take a closer look. "Hold on, I think I see it." He released his grip on the drawer and she stuck her hand into the gaping hole and fumbled around. She tugged on something, then pulled it free of the dresser.

Taylor pushed the drawer back into place. This time, it slid in as perfectly as the day it left the furniture store. It may have been scuffed, but the craftsmanship was solid, and he hoped they wouldn't have to throw it out. Things like this just weren't made like they used to be.

Next to him, Meg was using her sleeve to wipe off the front of a small book. "What is it?"

She held it close to her face and squinted at the words on the cover. "It looks like some sort of journal."

"Huh." Taylor took off his glove and touched the dark leather, his fingers leaving streaks on the surface. He wiped the dust off on his pants. "It could use some TLC." The book had to be at least fifty years old.

She eased it open, revealing pages filled with spidery black handwriting. "It's too dark in here to see. I'll take it home to check it out in better light."

She shut the book and placed it in her tote bag. They continued working on that corner of the building, moving a long dresser and two queen bed frames outside for further consideration. After a few hours, they'd finally cleared the entire floor in that section of the barn. Taylor stretched his arm out past deteriorating leather horse tack to pluck a pitchfork from its hook on the wall. A plethora of cobwebs came with it and a spider fled into a crack in the windowsill.

He cleaned the sticky silver strands off the tines and held it up next to him. "Do I look like a proper farmer now?"

She giggled. "You look like the guy in that painting."

"You mean American Gothic?" He pulled his dust

mask off, shaping his face into a more sober expression. "How about this?"

She laughed again. "Okay, I need to get a picture of this." She ran over to her bag and retrieved her phone, then snapped a photo. She looked at the image and grinned widely. "Perfect."

"Oh no, you're not getting off that easily," a woman's voice said from the open doorway. "You need to get in there too, Meg." They both looked up to see Zoe standing in the entrance. She didn't even try to hide the huge grin on her face. "C'mon," she demanded. "Hand over the phone and get in the picture. I'm not letting you out of this one."

Meg grumbled a little before giving Zoe her phone and returning to stand next to Taylor. "For the record, I hate having my picture taken."

"Hmm." Zoe peered at the image and frowned. "Something's not right." She stepped back through the open barn doors. "Come out here so you can stand in front of the barn, just like the couple in the painting."

Meg turned to Taylor and he shrugged. "I'm not telling Zoe no. I once told her it wasn't practical to serve something at a wedding and she insisted it could be done and would turn out amazing." He sighed, remembering how stubborn she'd been. "She was right."

Meg stared up at the rafters high overhead. "Fine." She stomped out of the barn.

They'd both worked with Zoe at the Lodge long enough to know it was easier to go along with what she wanted than to fight it.

When they were in position, Zoe finally took the picture. She examined the result and her face lit up. "I love it. Make sure you send me a copy, because that's going up on a wall somewhere once we get this place renovated." She handed the phone back to Meg.

Meg looked at the photo, then showed it to Taylor, who burst into laughter. "We look like we just tunneled out of a prison." Their clothes were covered in dust, and stray bits of hay stuck out from where they'd worked their way into his hair. He ran his fingers over his head and brushed the debris away.

"Eh. You look fine." Zoe gestured to the piles outside of the barn. "Looks like you're making some good progress."

Meg nodded. Now that she wasn't having her picture taken, her mood had improved. "We were hoping you'd take a look at the furnishings today and let us know what we should keep."

Zoe eyed the piles again. "How did all of this even fit in there?"

"I don't know, but that's only half of what we took out. The rest is in the dumpster." Meg gestured to the giant metal bin to the side of the barn.

"Well, I'll take a look at it before the end of the day," Zoe promised. "I actually came by to see if you were interested in having something to eat. Celia and I got out sandwich fixings. She's leaving soon to go shopping with a woman from church and Shawn and I are going to take a picnic down to the beach, but you're welcome to grab some lunch." She glanced at her watch. "I'd better get back. Shawn's got us on a tight schedule today."

Taylor smirked. Zoe's love of schedules and lists was well known, so it was much more likely that the schedule she'd referred to was of her own making. "Thanks. Lunch sounds great."

"Good. I'll see you later." Zoe looked at her watch again and hurried off.

"Are you ready to eat?" Meg asked Taylor.

"I could eat, but I'm not starved." His stomach grumbled loudly in protest and she gave him a pointed look.

"Okay, okay," he said sheepishly. He hadn't wanted to quit until she was ready to do so, but his body had betrayed him. "Maybe I'm hungrier than I thought."

They removed their work gloves and Meg looped the strap of her bag over her shoulder. As they emerged into full sunlight, Taylor took a few deep breaths, letting the salt-scented air clear the dust out of his lungs. Although he was no stranger to exercise, the muscles in his arms and legs were sending off signals that they'd be aching the next day.

"So, what do you think of the barn now?" Meg asked as they walked toward the Inn.

"I think we're making progress and it'll be a great space when we're done." He hesitated. "But there's a lot more to do."

"No kidding. I think it'll help once Shawn gets the tractor out. That thing takes up a ton of room." She sounded much more optimistic now than she had that morning.

She led him to a door at the back of the Inn. They used a boot scraper to clean off their dirty shoes, then entered the mud room, which led to the main part of the house.

"Wow, this place is huge." Taylor looked curiously at all of the closed doors lining the long hallway.

She laughed. "Well, it was built to be an inn, so I'd hope so. I can't imagine living here all by myself like Celia did for so many years. It seems much too big for just one person."

"Tell me about it," an elderly woman's voice carried down the hall from the kitchen.

Meg shot him a guilty look and whispered, "I didn't know she was still here."

They walked another ten feet, stopping when they reached a large kitchen decorated in various shades of blue that mimicked the waters of Willa Bay. It wouldn't have been Taylor's first choice of color, but it suited the surroundings.

Celia stood next to the sink with a cup of coffee in her hand. "Good afternoon. How is the barn cleanout going?"

"It's going well," Meg said. "Sorry about my comment about the Inn being too big for you. I didn't realize you were still here. Zoe said you went shopping."

Celia beamed at them. "Carla had to make a phone call first, but she'll be here soon. And you're totally right— I used to rattle around this place when I lived in it by myself. It's so nice to have Shawn and Zoe here all the time now." Her smile grew even wider. "And I'm really looking forward to having guests once the rooms are completed."

Taylor nodded, his gaze straying in the direction of the entry hall with its small check-in desk. "When will the first guests arrive?"

"The grand opening is in a few weeks, at the end of the month." Celia got plates out of the cupboard for them. "It's going to be wonderful to see the Inn so full of life again." Her face held a dreamy expression as she handed one to each of them, then gestured to the table. "Have as much as you'd like. We went a little overboard."

Zoe had told them that she and Celia had set out some sandwich fixings, but "some" was a gross understatement. Sliced tomatoes, huge leaves of bright-green romaine lettuce, rings of onions, and an assortment of deli meats and cheeses covered most of the table. A smaller platter held apple slices and baby carrots.

Taylor's eyes widened. "Okay, now I'm hungry."

His sandwich ended up being about six inches high, whereas hers was a more modest size. He'd built up quite an appetite after working all morning in the barn. They took their sandwiches, chips, fruit, veggies, and cans of soda out to the picnic table perched a safe distance back from the cliffside. Taylor imagined it would eventually be difficult to get a seat at one of the picnic tables, once the Inn started accommodating overnight guests. For now, though, the amenities were wonderfully uncrowded.

They sat side-by-side on the bench, facing the water. Zoe and Shawn were distant figures as they walked down the beach together.

"This is nice." Taylor took a deep breath and gazed out at the bay. "Back home, the sand is crammed with beachgoers and all of their gear. It's nice to have room to spread out here and actually enjoy being near the water." He took a deep breath of the salty air, which was simultaneously familiar and different from what he was accustomed to.

Meg finished a bite of her sandwich and set it down on her plate. "You're from Southern California, right?"

He nodded. "Yep. A suburb of San Diego." He popped the tab on his Coke and took a long swig of it.

"How'd you end up in Willa Bay?" she asked. "It's not exactly a booming metropolis."

He laughed. "Nope, that it's not. Actually, a friend of mine lives in Seattle and I came up to visit him. The restaurant I'd been working at had just closed down, so I was between jobs." He shrugged. "I heard about an opening at the Lodge, and when I interviewed for it, George hired me on the spot." He took a big bite of his sandwich, relishing how the bread, vegetables, deli meats, and cheeses came together to form something so simple, yet unbelievably delicious.

"Do you like it here?"

He swallowed, then looked at her. "Most of the time. I miss my family, and the surfing in Washington isn't great, but there are plenty of places to climb and I've gotten into hiking. The Northwest is pretty cool."

They sat in companionable silence while they ate their sandwiches. When she was finished, Meg carefully wiped off her hands and dug around in her bag.

She removed the journal and set it on the picnic table, opening it to the first page. Taylor looked on intently as he finished his food.

This journal belongs to Davina Carlsen, read an inscription on the first page.

"Davina Carlsen?" he said. "Do you think she was a guest at the resort?"

"I don't know," Meg said softly. She turned a few more pages, but the glare from the sun made it difficult to read the handwriting. The pages were sketchbook-style, devoid of any lines or guides for writing. Davina had made full use of the blank pages, decorating them with small sketches.

Meg tugged on Taylor's arm and pointed at the page. "Look at this."

He popped the last bit of carrot into his mouth, chewed, then wiped his hands on his pants before leaning in closer. "What is it?"

"She put recipes in her journal. It's too bright to see well, but she seems to have written about her life and must have been into cooking."

They both stared at the recipe, trying to make out the words.

"Golden Chicken?" Taylor read the recipe title out loud. "I've never heard of it."

She shrugged. "Must have been a specialty from those days." She scanned the top of the page for a date. "Looks like she wrote this during the 1920s."

"Can I see it?" he asked. "I love old recipes."

She passed him the book, taking care to not scrape the old leather on the picnic table. As he took it, his skin grazed hers, sending tingles through his fingertips and up into his arm. His gaze shot up and he momentarily took his eyes off the journal. The old leather hit the table. He fumbled to catch it, tearing a page in the process. She cringed as though she'd been physically injured.

He held the book in his hands, staring at in horror. "I'm sorry. I didn't mean to do that. It just slipped out of my hands."

"It's okay." She smiled at him. "It's not a big deal."

He ran his finger over the ripped paper. "I think I can tape this, if you'd like. I'm really sorry." Judging by the reverence she'd shown while handling the journal, it was obviously important to her. She'd only had it for a few hours and he'd already managed to ruin it.

She laid her hand on the rough table, a few inches away from his and looked him in the eyes. "Don't worry about it. I'll tape it when I get home. It's an old journal. I'm sure it's seen its share of war injuries. Besides, if it hadn't been for you helping me with the chest of drawers, it probably would have ended up in the dump."

A glimmer of a smile slid over his lips. He stood and gathered up their plates and empty cans of soda. "Maybe we should get back to work in the barn. Who knows how many more journals are lost in that mess?"

She laughed. "Maybe we'll find a whole set of them."

They didn't find any more journals, but they did sort

through a previously untouched corner of the barn. It felt like they were making progress. Zoe came by to help Meg make decisions about which furniture to throw out and which was good enough to move back into the barn until they could work on it. Moving things back in felt like they were going the wrong direction, but it still looked better than it had that morning.

"Thanks, Taylor." Meg took her work gloves off and wiped her hand over her brow. "I really appreciate your help. I think we're getting somewhere now."

"No problem." Taylor took his own gloves off and handed them to her.

"You know, you should really be out having fun on your days off, not helping me." Her back was turned to him as she put both pairs of dirty gloves into a plastic sack and then tossed them into her bag.

He raised an eyebrow. "Fun like what?" There weren't exactly a lot of things to do or people to hang out with on Monday and Tuesday, his customary days off from his job at the Lodge. When he took vacation time, he usually went home to see his family in California.

She picked up her bag and, rubbing the worn leather strap between her thumb and forefinger, turned to face him. "I don't know. Like spend time with friends? You said you like hiking and climbing. Maybe go out on a date with a nice girl."

He cocked his head to the side. "And just where am I supposed to meet this 'nice' girl? We don't get a lot of singles frequenting the Lodge, except for weddings, and there's no way I'm going to ask out a wedding guest. The single women at weddings can be a little crazy sometimes." He wasn't sure why he was even talking about this with Meg. They didn't usually discuss his love life, or lack thereof, although she'd sometimes relayed information about her dates with Theo.

Blood pounded lightly in his ears. He wished she *wouldn't* tell him about Theo. That guy didn't seem right for Meg, although she seemed to like him a lot.

They walked out of the barn and she slid the door closed. While they were making their way back to the Inn, she snapped her fingers. "Hey, what about my sister, Samantha? You guys would be great together."

He gritted his teeth. He'd thought she was done with this, but he should have known better.

"Sam loves to do outdoor stuff and she doesn't have a normal schedule, at least for the next week. You should totally ask her out." Out of the corner of his eye, he saw her look up at him, but he pretended not to see. "I really think you should get out more."

He sighed. She was like a dog with a bone. "I don't know. I don't have time for dating." His last relationship, with a woman he'd met through his friend in Seattle, had fizzled out over a year ago. They'd both been wrapped up in their careers and hadn't made enough of an effort to see each other. Eventually, it had just been easier to let their relationship go.

She grinned. "No problem. Sam just got out of a long-term relationship and isn't looking for anything serious either. I think you should ask her out. Honestly, you'd be doing us all a favor. She seems a little lost after her breakup. She could use some fun, especially with a nice guy like you."

A nice guy. He knew she'd meant it in a good way, but the words still stung. Was that all she thought of him? He quickened his pace. The faster they got to the Inn's parking lot, the faster he could escape this conversation and drive home in peace.

She jogged to keep up with him. "Why are you so against having a little fun? Are you scared?"

He stopped and ran his hand over the top of his head, picking out a stray piece of hay. "No, I'm not scared." The hay floated to the ground as Meg bounced impatiently, waiting for him to complete his thoughts.

When he didn't continue, she said, "Look, I'm not trying to be annoying, but working in a restaurant is a high-pressure job. You need to have an outlet to blow off a little steam. That's the only reason I mention it. You should do something outside of work." She put her hand on his arm and he gritted his teeth to keep from thinking about it. "I didn't realize until I started dating Theo how focused I was on work. It's been good for me to get out of my comfort zone."

Is that what her relationship with Theo was? A way to get out of her comfort zone? Were Meg and Theo not as serious as he'd thought? His eyes glazed over as he replayed everything she'd ever told him about her boyfriend.

"Hey. Are you okay?"

He shook his head to clear it. Meg's relationship with Theo wasn't any of his business.

"Yeah, I'm good. Talking about work reminded me that I need to submit our meat order for next week."

She shot him a funny look, but didn't question him. "See, I told you that you need to have some outside interests. On your day off, you shouldn't be thinking about a meat order that's a week away."

He nodded. "You're right." He shouldn't be analyzing his friend's relationship either. "Check with your sister and find out if she'd be interested in going out with me. Maybe I do need a distraction outside of work, and it sounds like she could use some casual fun too."

She nodded vigorously, the exertion flushing her cheeks so prettily that he couldn't take his eyes off of her. "I'll talk to her." She gave him a quick hug that he didn't see coming. "I think the two of you are really going to hit it off."

He started walking again, trying to forget the feeling of her body pressed up against his. "I hope so." His heart was obviously confused by their friendship, and meeting someone new could be the recipe for change that he needed so badly.

10

Meg

Make a roux with flour and butter, then add milk and chicken broth, Meg copied the instructions from the journal onto a 3x5-inch index card. She squinted to make out the rest of the recipe. *Stir constantly until thickened.* Golden Chicken seemed like a fairly simple recipe, but it wasn't something she'd ever made before.

She, Zoe, Shawn, and Celia had decided months ago that they'd have a 1920s theme for the Inn's grand opening, and she'd decided to prepare some of the recipes from the journal. It seemed like fate that she and Taylor had discovered the journal and its recipes just in time for the big event. Maybe the dishes she'd chosen to cook wouldn't go over well with modern-day diners, but the vintage recipes would add a dash of flair and authenticity to the party. Besides, cooking the unfamiliar dishes took her mind off of the situation with the barn and gave her an opportunity to contribute something of her own to the grand opening.

Since she couldn't cook in her own restaurant yet, her mom's catering kitchen was the next best thing. Her mom and sisters would be in sometime after noon to start preparations for the rest of the food for the grand opening. Most of the food Willa Bay Provisions would be serving would be from their regular menu, but they'd also be offering the Golden Chicken, Baked Rice Milanaise, and an icebox cake—all recipes from the journal. Meg had asked Taylor if he was interested in helping her out before his shift at the Lodge, but he'd hemmed and hawed, and she wasn't sure if he'd show up or not. He'd seemed interested in the journal too, so she'd been surprised at his reluctance to try out the recipes in person.

Someone rapped on the exterior door. Meg marked her place with a notecard and carefully closed the old book. She opened the door and found Taylor standing there, shifting on his feet.

"Hey," she said warmly. "I wasn't sure I'd see you today."

"I wasn't sure either," he mumbled, not quite meeting her gaze. "I had a lot to do this morning."

"Well, thanks for coming. I'm a little worried about how these recipes are going to taste and I'd love to get your input on them." She gestured to the center island. "C'mon. Let me show you which ones I chose. I saw at least thirty recipes scattered throughout the book, but these looked like they'd be best for the event."

She hadn't finished reading the journal—so far, she'd only made it about halfway through. Reading Davina's private thoughts seemed like something she should savor and not rush. Meg still hadn't figured out if Davina had been a guest or an employee at the resort, but she hoped the journal would reveal her identity soon.

Meg showed Taylor her selections and he familiarized

himself with the instructions. She stood next to him, reading over his shoulder, although she'd already gone over the recipes about twenty times to ensure she had everything to prepare them.

"Seems easy enough." He looked directly into her eyes, his face mere inches away from her. "Are you sure you need my help?" His voice held an unfamiliar edge.

Caught off-guard, she moved to the other side of the island to put some distance between them. Why was Taylor acting like this? Had she overstepped the bounds of their friendship by asking him to help today—especially after he'd already been so generous with his time?

"I suppose I don't *need* your help, but I thought you might enjoy testing out some of the recipes in the journal." She paused to gauge his reaction, but his face was stoic. "If you don't have time, I completely understand."

A muscle twitched in his neck and he sighed deeply, then gave her a small smile. "I have time." He removed his lightweight jacket and hung it on a hook on the wall, then surveyed the room. "Do you have an extra apron?"

Meg grinned. "I do." She grabbed a red apron off the wall. It bore the words "Kiss the Cook" and an image of a frog. Her mom loved novelty aprons and kept a few in the catering kitchen.

He read the front of it and his cheeks flushed to almost the same shade as the apron. He held it out at arm's length. "Do you have a different one?"

His expression was priceless. There were others, but she wasn't going to tell him that. She pressed her lips together to keep from laughing, then managed to say with a straight face, "Nope, that's the only extra we have."

He took another look at it, then slipped it over his

head and tied the strings at the waist. Meg couldn't keep quiet once she saw it on him, and a giggle escaped. He looked far different than he did at the Lodge, where he always dressed professionally in a crisp, white chef's jacket.

He pursed his lips and glared up at the ceiling. However, when his gaze lowered, he broke into a huge smile. She breathed a sigh of relief. The gag apron had melted some of the tension between them, and she hoped they'd revert to their normal camaraderie in the kitchen.

Her plan entailed making all three of the new recipes in the morning and sampling them at an early lunch. The icebox cake was the first thing she'd made when she'd arrived at the kitchen over an hour ago. It was supposed to be in the freezer for several hours before serving, and though she wasn't sure whether it would be completely frozen by lunch time, it should still be edible.

If any of the recipes turned out badly, there were always the tried-and-true catering selections to fall back on. But, if their initial attempts tasted good, she and Taylor would prepare them in larger quantities for the party. With any luck, it would be the latter case. There was a lot riding on the grand opening, and she wanted the Inn's food to make a good impression from the start.

She'd already seasoned the raw chicken breasts with salt and pepper and put them in the oven, so she got straight to work preparing the roux for the Golden Chicken while Taylor focused on the Baked Rice Milanaise.

He eyed the recipe card. "Are you sure people are going to like this? It's not fancy."

She shrugged, her own doubts resurfacing. "I don't know, but Davina's notes said it was a popular dish. If nothing else, it'll add a nice historical element to the party."

When the oven timer rang, she pulled the chicken out and set it on a rack to cool before slicing. She returned to her sauce, finishing it with an egg yolk and a splash of lemon, then seasoning to taste.

Across the wide table, Taylor's knife flashed through the tough skin of a green pepper, sending minced bits of vegetable into a pile on the cutting board. Without looking up, he said, "You're chopping the onion, right?"

"What onion?" Her chicken dish didn't call for any onion.

"Oh." He chuckled as he swept the small pieces of vegetable into a bowl. "I'm so used to us working together in the kitchen. I totally forgot we were making different things."

She laughed. "No problem. I'm actually almost done with this, so I'll put it in the warmer and then get started on the onions." She pointed the wire whisk at him, and teased, "But remember, I'm the head chef in this kitchen."

He grinned and saluted her. "Yes, ma'am."

She minced the onions for Taylor's dish and brought the cutting board over to the stove, where he was just adding the green peppers to some olive oil he'd heated in a frying pan. He dumped the onions in and stirred. Delicious aromas wafted upward from the mixture.

He sniffed the air appreciatively, "You know, you just can't go wrong with onions and green pepper."

"I agree." She smiled. It was nice being back in the kitchen with him, working in tandem. When she'd been employed at the Lodge, they'd always had the innate ability to communicate without words while creating amazing food for their guests. She missed that sense of closeness.

Once the peppers and onions were soft, he mixed them with the rice he'd boiled on another burner. He then threw in a few final ingredients, scooped everything into a casserole dish, and popped it into the oven for a quick bake.

While it was cooking, Meg set a table for two tucked into the corner of the kitchen. Taylor moved the cutting board and knife to the sink, then wiped down the counter, his long arms sweeping across the stainless-steel surface like it was no bigger than the table she was setting. He continued cleaning the other areas they'd used as she loaded the dishwasher. When the rice dish was ready, he took it out of the oven and set the bubbling casserole on a trivet at the table.

He eyed it dubiously. "Well, at least it smells good."

"I'm sure it will be fantastic." She put a few slices of chicken on a couple of plates, then ladled the aptly named golden sauce over the meat and brought the plates to the table.

Taylor inserted a serving spoon into the rice concoction, releasing a cloud of lightly scented steam that made Meg's mouth water in anticipation. They sat down across from each other and he served up two hearty portions of rice.

"Bon appétit!" Taylor said before cutting into his chicken. He lifted it to his mouth and held it there for a few seconds, breathing in its aroma like he was tasting a fine wine. He chewed, then swallowed. "Hey, this is really good."

"Is it?" Meg tasted the rice dish. "Actually, this is too." She ate a few bites of chicken, making sure to liberally coat it with sauce to get the full effect. She set her fork down and regarded Taylor. "Have you ever considered we might be food snobs?"

He laughed, his eyes twinkling merrily. "We're definitely food snobs." He pointed his fork at his plate. "But I'd serve these in my restaurant any day. Davina was onto something with her recipes." His gaze flickered over to the casserole dish. "However, the presentation leaves a lot to be desired. For the party, we can serve this in small bowls, but if I was serving this at the Lodge, I'd probably make each portion individually in its own porcelain ramekin."

"I agree." Meg couldn't help but wonder what other treasures the journal held. Every time she read a few pages, it was like stepping back in time, into Davina's life. It must have been fascinating to experience the Inn during its heyday. Had Davina made these same recipes for its guests back then?

Taylor cleared the dishes from the table and Meg got up to make a pot of coffee to drink with dessert, still thinking about the journal. Back in Davina's time, all of the food at the Inn had been prepared in the same kitchen Celia had used for most of her life. Meg, accustomed to working in larger restaurant kitchens, couldn't imagine cooking large quantities of food in such a small space. Although they didn't plan to use the Inn's kitchen for large-scale cooking on a regular basis, Meg had lent her knowledge and years of experience to design the renovation of it for efficiency.

Once the coffee was percolating noisily into the pot, Meg took the icebox cake out of the freezer. As she'd suspected, it hadn't frozen completely, but she was still able to slice off two pieces without it falling apart. She put the rest of the cake back to allow it to finish freezing. Later, she'd offer some to her mom and sisters to see what they thought.

With fresh coffee and cake in front of them, Meg and

Taylor sat back down at the table. "Are these Oreos?" Taylor asked as he cut into his dessert with the side of his fork.

"Yup." She watched him closely, hoping he'd like it.

"I didn't realize they had Oreos back then. I always assumed they were a more recent invention." He took a big bite and chewed thoughtfully.

"I didn't either. Apparently, they've been around since 1912. Who knew?" She ate a forkful of the chilled cake, letting the morsel of creamy chocolate treat rest on her tastebuds. Ordinarily, she wasn't much of a baker, but this hadn't involved an oven, so was it even considered baking? Whatever the case, it was tasty—but she hadn't met many sweets that she didn't enjoy. "What do you think?"

He looked up from his plate and took a sip of coffee before responding. "It's good. Not too sugary. I think it'll be refreshing on a hot day."

Relief flooded over her. All three of the recipes were a success. "It's supposed to be in the high seventies tomorrow." She took another bite. It could use a little more vanilla, but that was the only thing she planned to tweak for serving it at the grand opening.

"Good." He stared at her and his lips quivered like he was trying not to laugh. Suddenly, he reached across the table.

The world came to a stop as he brushed the rough pad of his thumb over her cheek, the pleasurable sensation sending a warmth down her neck and into her spine. When she recovered, she shot him a quizzical look.

The color had drained from his complexion. "I'm so sorry. I don't know why I did that. There were crumbs on your face and I thought it was funny and..." He shook his head. "I don't know what I was thinking."

She responded quickly, trying to stop him from

spiraling. "It's fine. I totally understand. I'm always embarrassing my family with how messily I eat. I'm sure any of them would have done the same."

"But I'm not someone in your family." He avoided making eye contact with her as he drained his coffee, jumped to his feet and set the plate and cup in the sink. "I'd better get going. I forgot I need to take care of some administrative tasks at the Lodge before the dinner rush starts."

She jumped up from her chair. "Oh, of course. Thank you so much for being my guinea pig."

"You're welcome." Taylor removed his apron and hung it back on the hook, swapping it out for his jacket. He was at least ten paces ahead of her as he exited the kitchen, the door clicking shut behind him.

Meg stared at the exit, her vision glazing over. Taylor had been running hot and cold lately. One minute he was the sweet, funny guy she'd known for a couple of years, and the next, he was so standoffish that they might have been strangers. Something was bothering him, and she hoped his generosity in giving up his free time to help her wasn't contributing to it.

She busied herself with chopping vegetables and making ten more rectangular icebox cakes, so they'd be properly frozen before serving tomorrow. They couldn't do everything the day before the event, but the more they did do ahead of time, the easier it would come together the next morning. It would have been nice to have had Taylor's help, but she understood he had other obligations.

At one o'clock, Libby and Debbie arrived, with Samantha hot on their heels.

Debbie took a deep breath. "It smells wonderful in

here." She gestured to the counter. "Is this one of the recipes out of that book you found?"

Meg nodded. "Taylor and I tried three things from the journal, and they were all excellent. I'm finishing up the prep for them and they should be fairly simple to put together tomorrow."

Libby took a three-ring binder out of her giant purse and sat down at the table with it. "We've got a lot to do before tomorrow too."

"I'm happy to help," Meg said.

"Doesn't Zoe need you at the Inn?" Debbie asked from the sink where she'd been washing her hands. She dried off on a paper towel and tossed it into the garbage, then came over to the counter to stand next to Meg.

"No. She said she and Tia had everything under control." Meg uttered a self-deprecating laugh. "I think I just get underfoot when I'm there."

Libby looked up from her notes. "I'm sure that's not true."

"Oh, but I think it is." Meg laughed again, but, in truth, it bothered her that they didn't need her at the Inn.

"Well, we're glad to have you here with us," Debbie said warmly. She walked over to Libby and peered over her shoulder. "What's first on the agenda?"

Libby flipped a page in her binder and scanned its contents. "This menu is heavy on hors d'oeuvres that we'll put together right before the event, but there are things to get done today. Let's get started with the deviled eggs."

"I'm on it." Samantha disappeared into the walk-in refrigerator and returned with two massive cartons of eggs. She set them down near the stove and filled a stock pot with water from the sink.

"How are you doing, Mom?" Meg asked. With everything going on at the Inn, she hadn't talked to her mother since the family dinner on Sunday. Even then, things had been so chaotic that having a private conversation with anyone had been difficult.

Debbie looked up and shrugged. "I've been better." Pink circles of blusher stood out from her cheeks in stark contrast to the pallor of the rest of her skin.

"Are you feeling alright?" Meg held her breath. Her mom had been so sick two years ago. Now, Meg panicked a little every time Debbie had even the slightest cold.

"I'm not ill, if that's what you're worried about." Debbie poked her finger at something on the page in front of Libby. "I'll get started on this." She disappeared into the walk-in cooler.

"What's going on with Mom?" Meg hissed to her sisters. "Is there something she's not telling me?"

Samantha sighed. "One of her friends from her cancer group died."

Meg felt a rush of relief, followed by a stronger wave of guilt. She was glad to know that her mom was healthy, but another family hadn't been so fortunate.

Libby came over to Meg. "She's taking it pretty hard."

"Well, wouldn't you be?" Sam asked. "I wish I'd never told her to go to that knitting club meeting." She removed a bin of flour from the pantry and slammed it down on the counter. Little clouds of flour dust floated off the lid, settling on all of the surfaces below.

"It wouldn't have changed anything," Libby said.

"Maybe not, but then I wouldn't have to feel so guilty. Mom's down in the dumps now and it's all my fault." Sam swiped at the flour with a clean towel, brushing it into the trash.

Libby rolled her eyes. "Again, it's not your fault. Not everything is about you."

They'd obviously known about the death of their

mom's friend for a while, but nobody had told Meg about it. She lived above her parents' garage and yet was the last to know. It seemed like she was always just outside of the loop for everything in her life.

Debbie came out of the walk-in, carrying an armful of produce. Meg and Libby helped her to unload it onto the counter, while Sam finished cleaning up the flour mess.

Meg eyed her mother. Should she say anything to her about her friend's death? It didn't seem like the right time —Debbie was smiling now, in her element as she scurried around the kitchen.

Meg had hoped to have a nice relaxing day, trying out the journal recipes and spending time with her family. Instead, she'd somehow upset Taylor, and now had her mom to worry about too. On the bright side, the dishes she'd cooked had turned out great and she'd get to serve them at the event tomorrow—and maybe again when she opened her own restaurant at the Inn. Although, with the lack of major progress in emptying the barn, she wouldn't be cooking there anytime soon. Thinking about that made her almost as depressed as her mom had been earlier.

Very little in her life was going right, and the only thing that would take her mind off of everything was to immerse herself in the thing she loved best—cooking.

She locked eyes with Libby and rolled up her sleeves. "I'm sure we have a lot to do today. What can I do first?"

11

Tia

"I love your dress," Tia said to Celia as she climbed the stairs to the Inn at Willa Bay's front porch and joined her by the railing. "You look like you just stepped out of the pages of a 1920s Sears catalog." For the themed grand opening of the Inn at Willa Bay, the elderly woman wore a new, cap-sleeved floral dress in a shade of blue that matched her eyes, and black patent-leather Mary Janes on her feet.

"Why thank you." Celia preened, patting the snow-white curls pinned tightly against her scalp. "You look wonderful, yourself."

"Thanks." Tia beamed at the compliment. She'd had a hard time deciding what to wear, but had settled on a sleeveless, fiery red dress in a simple drop-waist style, with a gold sash that tied just under her natural waist. She swirled the skirt, loving the way the fabric swished around her legs and fell just below the knees. She'd bought a new pair of period-appropriate heels for the party, but had returned them to the store. Her own comfortable black pumps may not have been as authentic, but she'd be walking around all day over uneven ground. The grand opening had enough going on as it was—they didn't need to be rushing her to the emergency room with a broken ankle. "Are you ready for the crowds?"

"I've never been more ready," Celia said. "I can't wait for the whole town to see all of the hard work everyone has put into the renovations." She leaned on the top of the railing for support and scanned the grounds with pride. Workers scurried around the neatly manicured lawn, rolling round tables into place. Zoe stood near the newly remodeled gazebo, supervising the setup. "It's been so long since everything looked like this. After my husband died, I couldn't keep up with all of the maintenance. I hated seeing how bad things got." A far-off look appeared in her eyes, as though she was reliving memories from long ago. She stood a little straighter and grabbed hold of her walker. "The Olsen family would be so delighted to see how the resort looks now."

"I'm sure they would. Is anyone from their family attending the party today?" The Olsen family had owned the Inn before Celia took over, but Tia didn't know much about them. With the grandeur of the Inn and the lovely grounds overlooking the bay, the resort must have been extremely popular back in its day. It would be fascinating to locate some old photographs of weddings here to see how they compared to modern-day events. Once things settled down, she hoped to learn more about the Inn's history, either from Celia or by digging through records at the local historical society.

Although she'd grown up halfway across the United States, the history of Willa Bay and the Inn, itself, intrigued Tia. The town had enjoyed so much prosperity in the early 1900s, but fell from popularity as air travel became more prevalent. Without a campaign from the Willa Bay Chamber of Commerce in the 1970s, it would have become just another town that was a ghost of its former self. Instead, it had undergone a renaissance, and now thrived on tourism and the wedding industry. The Inn's grand opening was its own chance for rebirth, and Tia intended to help ensure its success.

A wave of uncertainty swept over her. Reporters from the local papers would be in attendance and Zoe had sent invitations to some of the national bridal magazines. This afternoon was a big deal that could make or break the Inn's future, and as one of two people coordinating the event, some of that responsibility fell on Tia's shoulders.

Her mother's words echoed in her head. *You've never been the responsible type.* Was she right? Could Tia handle this much pressure?

Celia smiled sadly and shook her head, drawing Tia's attention back to the present. "No, the Olsens didn't have any children, which is why they left the Inn to me. They knew I'd take care of it for them." She glanced back at the hectic scene on the lawn. "I may have let them down in that regard after Charlie died, but I think I've redeemed myself now."

Tia wrapped an arm around Celia's shoulders. "I think they would be very happy with how everything has turned out." A movement caught Tia's eye. Zoe was beckoning for her. "I've got to get to work, but I'll see you later, okay?"

Celia nodded, then gestured to her walker. "I may not be able to buzz around here anymore as quickly as you girls do, but if there's anything I can help with, please let me know."

Tia laughed. "You've got the most important job at all.

We need someone to greet the guests as they arrive to keep things from getting too chaotic. Make sure they sign the memory book too."

"This isn't my first rodeo." Celia grinned. "I'll make sure all of the guests are taken care of." Celia, who would continue to reside in the owner's suite of the Inn, was tasked with putting her engaging personality and true love for the business to work as a guest liaison once the Inn opened for overnight stays.

"I know you will." Tia looked over at Zoe. "I'd better go before Zoe has a conniption fit."

"Me too," Celia snickered. "I love that girl, but she can be scarily efficient at times." She pointed her walker at the gently sloped ramp leading to the lawn, where a table and chair waited for her near the entrance.

Tia watched her for a few seconds, then hurried down the short flight of stairs and over to where Zoe was waiting for her at the gazebo.

"Hey." Zoe looked up from her iPad. Unlike Tia and Celia, she was still dressed casually, wearing a pair of blue jeans and a sleeveless button-down blouse that tied just below the waist. Not exactly a vision of the 1920s. "How are you doing?"

Tia smiled. "I'm doing fine." She may have been a bundle of nerves inside, but she wasn't going to let her boss know that. This event was too important to everyone involved with the Inn to let a little self-doubt get in her way. "What's up?"

"I need you to supervise the setup while I change into my dress. I left it in one of the guest rooms so I could save a few minutes by getting dressed there rather than running back to my cottage to change." Zoe scanned the grounds, her expression imperceptible behind the dark lenses of her sunglasses. "Everything seems to be on track here, so I think this is a good time for me to slip away."

Tia checked her watch. "The guests are due to arrive in thirty minutes and there are always early birds. You'd better get going. I've got this." Her nerves were starting to subside and the negative thoughts in her head had cleared. Managing events put her into a state of calm focus that she hadn't experienced in school or any other part of her life.

Zoe removed her sunglasses and rubbed her eyes, revealing dark circles under them. "Okay." She replaced her sunglasses and looked directly at Tia. "There's so much riding on today." Her voice wobbled uncharacteristically, and Tia feared her boss was about to break into tears.

She looked at Zoe more closely. "Did you sleep at all last night?"

Zoe shrugged. "Maybe an hour?" Her shoulders slumped. "I couldn't fall asleep. All of these scenarios of things that could go wrong kept running through my head."

Tia touched her arm to make sure she had Zoe's attention. "You've got this. The Inn is amazing, and everyone is going to absolutely love it. Now go get dressed!"

Zoe swallowed hard, then nodded. "Okay." She walked a few steps toward the Inn, then rushed back to hand Tia the iPad. "I forgot to give you this." She paused, and her voice wavered again. "And Tia?"

"Yeah?"

"Thank you." She smiled at Tia. "I don't know if I could have managed all of this without you."

"No problem." As her boss walked away, Tia tapped on the iPad screen to wake it up but didn't look at it immediately. Usually, Zoe was the most put-together, Type-A person that Tia had ever met. If even the unflappable Zoe could fall apart sometimes, maybe there was hope for Tia yet.

She'd managed to tick off a few more boxes on Zoe's checklist when one of the event staff, dressed in black pants and a white shirt, burst into her line of sight.

The young woman was out of breath and had to compose herself before speaking. "Zoe needs you. She's freaking out."

Tia's alert level shot up to a Code Red. When Zoe left twenty minutes ago, she'd been rattled, but not anywhere near a panicked state. "What's wrong?"

The woman took another deep breath, then let her words pour out. "There's a leak in one of the bathrooms upstairs. I was making coffee in those big urns in the kitchen and I heard her calling out. I tried to get Shawn, but I can't find him anywhere."

Shawn may have gone back to his cottage to change into his party clothes. Tia gave her a reassuring smile. "Thanks for letting me know. I'll go check on her."

The woman nodded and scurried off, happy to be relieved of her burden. Tia jogged over to the Inn, took the stairs two at a time, and flung open the door. Days like this were why sensible shoes were a necessity.

"Zoe?" she called up the staircase to the second floor.

"I'm up here!"

Tia ran up the long flight of stairs and stepped directly into a stream of water snaking its way along the non-carpeted portion of the hardwood-lined hallway. Her heart sank. This wasn't good.

She followed the trail of water to the room at the end of the hallway. In the attached bath, Zoe knelt in a puddle, frantically attempting to mop up the mess with their brand-new, fluffy white guest towels. She'd wrapped another towel around a pipe linking to the pedestal sink, but it hadn't done much to stem the flow of water.

"Where's Shawn?" Zoe swiped her hand over her head to smooth back all of the hair that had fallen out of her once-neat ponytail. "I need him." She might have been mostly fine earlier, but now she was now in a full-on panic. Tears streamed down her face, dripping onto her soaked blouse and jeans like little tributaries leading to the river.

Tia shook her head. "I don't know." She whipped out her cell phone and called the number for the emergency plumber that she'd programmed into her contacts. After getting their assurance that they'd be there within fifteen minutes, she stopped to assess the situation.

"Did you try the shut-off valve?"

"It's stuck." Zoe uttered a harsh laugh. "I came in here to get dressed, but discovered a flood instead. Of course this would happen on the most important day of my life."

Tia's heart hammered in her chest as she reached forward to try her luck with the handle on the valve. It refused to budge. "It'll be okay." She wasn't sure she believed that herself, but Zoe needed the reassurance. *Think, Tia!* Water sprayed out of the pipe, and she winced at the dark splotches forming on the skirt of her dress. *It's only water. It will dry.* However, dry seemed a far-off concept at the moment.

Tia snapped her fingers. "Hold on." She exited the bathroom and tried the handle on the door to the supply closet. It was supposed to be locked, but it turned easily. Luckily, Zoe hadn't done her final walkthrough yet to make sure the second floor was ready for the partygoers to explore.

The party. She checked her watch again. Less than five minutes until the guests were scheduled to arrive.

She yanked on the doorknob and the door swung open on well-greased hinges. Shawn's toolbag lay open on the floor, right where it had been last week when he'd asked her to fetch him a flathead screwdriver to tighten up a chair in the living room.

She grabbed a pair of pliers from the jumble of tools and ran back to the bathroom. Zoe hadn't moved and her face had taken on an air of sad acceptance. Tia clenched the jaws of the pliers around the shut off valve and applied downward pressure, jiggling it a little. Finally, it gave. She dropped the pliers and turned the valve handle until it met resistance.

They stared at the leak. The jet of water slowed and became a mere trickle. They both uttered loud sighs of relief, then looked at each other and laughed. It was a scene straight out of a comedy, but Tia was having a hard time finding the rest of the situation humorous. Even with Zoe's best attempts to keep the water at bay with towels, she'd only captured about a third of it.

"What are we going to do?" Zoe whispered, her eyes wide as she absorbed the scene in front of her.

Tia took charge. She helped Zoe up off of the floor. "This is your big day. You are going to put on your pretty dress, then go out there and greet everyone who's come to celebrate with you. I'll wait for the plumber and see if I can get this mess taken care of."

Zoe looked like she was about to protest, but had a change of heart. She closed her eyes for a moment, then opened them. "Okay." She shut the bathroom door halfway and reached for a garment bag hanging on the door. "Thank you, Tia." She smiled slightly. "I feel like I'm already saying that a lot today. You've been a big help here at the Inn, and an even better friend. So, thank you—for everything."

Tia had been about to duck out of the room to retrieve more towels from the linen closet, but Zoe's words stopped her in her tracks. They meant a lot to her. She'd been in Willa Bay for almost half a year, but hadn't made many friends. Her cheeks burned from the praise and she stared down at the floor. "Of course."

"I'd give you a hug, but I don't think you'd want that." Zoe glanced down ruefully at her sodden clothing. "Your dress is gorgeous. I hope it'll be okay."

"It'll be fine. For real, though, go get dressed. Someone has to mingle with the guests." She gave Zoe a nudge, and followed her out the door.

Zoe ducked into one of the rooms to change while Tia hurried to the linen closet at the end of the hall. The spotless, fluffy white towels they'd purchased to create a spa experience at the Inn weren't ideal for mopping up water, but they were nearby. Right now, availability counted the most. They had to get everything as dry as possible before the water leaked through the floorboards. An image of water dripping onto partygoers in the living room below flashed across her mind and she sped up her work.

Before Zoe left, she stopped in the bathroom to check on Tia. "I'm heading downstairs, but I'm going to put one of those quilt racks in the hallway to block off this part of the Inn. That way, people can still go in some of the rooms up here and get a feel for the place." Her gaze swept over the bathroom. "Wow. You're almost done. I mopped up the water in the hall, so I think we've managed to avert a bigger crisis. I hope the plumber comes soon."

Tia eyed her watch. "They should be here in a few

minutes." She smiled at Zoe. "You look fantastic. I love all of these 1920s dresses."

"Me too." Zoe peered at herself in the bathroom mirror, adjusted the sleeves on her mauve wrap dress, then smoothed the top of three tiers on the skirt that fell just below the knee. "I could get used to dressing like this every day. I feel like a princess."

Tia laughed and looked at her own reflection. The damp splotches on her red dress had paled now, and even in the harsh light, the bright fabric set off her dark hair nicely. Although she diligently applied sunscreen on a daily basis, her naturally brown skin glowed with an added layer of richness from the summer sun. She dabbed at a tiny smear of mascara next to her eyelid, then grinned at Zoe in the mirror. "This party is going to be amazing."

Zoe put her hands on Tia's shoulders from behind and leaned in, beaming. "We need a photo of us."

Tia looked around. "Here? In the bathroom?"

Zoe laughed. "Yeah, why not? We'll have formal photos later with Celia, Meg, and Shawn, but this is definitely something to remember." She pulled out her phone and they carefully maneuvered around the soggy towels strewn about the floor to stand against the white subway-tiled wall. Zoe held her arm out long enough to take a picture of both of them, and said, "Say flooding!"

"Flooding!" Tia snickered, composed herself, and smiled at the phone.

Zoe snapped the shot, then gathered up all of her belongings. "I'd better get going before they wonder what happened to me! I'll send someone up to take care of the towels and finish cleaning up. I don't want you to ruin your dress. You've put as much work into this party as any of us."

Tia nodded, warming with gratitude that her efforts had been recognized. "I'll stay here until the plumber comes, okay?"

"Okay, but make sure you leave as soon as he gets here!" Zoe waggled her finger at Tia. "I don't want you to miss out."

Tia smothered a grin. Zoe had made a full recovery from her brief mental breakdown and was back to her old, bossy self. "Yes, ma'am."

Zoe hurried out of the room, clutching her wet clothes which she'd wrapped up in the plastic garment bag. Tia picked up the soggy towels and dumped them in the bathtub so the plumber would have room to work.

"I can do that," a man from the event staff said from behind her. "I'll just take these down to the laundry." He grabbed a huge armload of used towels and disappeared.

With most of the evidence of a water leak gone, the bathroom looked almost normal. Tia let herself lean against the tiled wall and close her eyes for a moment. This could have been a lot worse than it was, but they'd managed to keep things fairly under control. *See, Mom,* she thought. *I can handle responsibility.*

Her eyes popped open. Even after being away from her family for half a year, she still couldn't get her mom's voice out of her head. It wasn't that she didn't love her parents, but constantly being around their judgmental treatment of her hadn't been good for her mental health. Although there were things she missed about living in Texas, including her family, she was better off in Willa Bay.

The plumber arrived and made short work of the leak. With the quilt rack barricading the rooms at the end of the hall and her dress now completely dried, it was as if nothing had happened. Tia went downstairs, smiling at the women perched on the living room sofas. Some wore period dresses, others were just wearing their Sunday best. All of them appeared to be having the time of their lives.

Over at the catering tent, she found Meg hiding near the canvas side flaps. Unsurprisingly, Meg had chosen a simple, unadorned dress in a brilliant shade of emerald green that draped at the waist and flowed to mid-calf. It looked comfortable, yet functional, while still being thematically appropriate.

"Hey," Tia whispered. "What are you doing?"

Meg peered intently at the guests sitting at the tables covered with blue-checkered tablecloths, her face pale. "Do you think they like the food?"

Tia followed her gaze. People were smiling and laughing as they shoveled food into their mouths from white paper plates. It had been decided that, for this event, they could do without fancier tableware in favor of a casual, picnic style, especially since guests might want to walk around and explore the grounds as they ate.

"I'd say they love it." She took a closer look at Meg. Did everyone have opening-day jitters? "Why are you so worried? Everyone always loves your cooking."

Meg sighed. "Yeah, but those are tried-and-true recipes. I took these ones out of that journal I found. I have no idea if people will like them."

Tia stared out at the eating area again. "Um, I think they like it." She pointed at a table consisting of two middle-aged couples. "They're practically licking their plates clean."

The tension in Meg's face eased. "Do you really think so?"

"Yes," Tia said firmly. She clutched Meg's arm and

tugged on it to pull her way from the tent. "Now go mingle!"

Meg took a deep breath, then let her lips slide into a huge smile. "Thanks." She took a few tentative steps, squared her shoulders, and walked purposefully over to a table to greet the occupants.

Tia roamed the event, helping guests find each other, answering questions, and checking to make sure everything was still fine with the problematic bathroom. At the end of the day, she was more exhausted than she'd ever been after an event.

When the final guest left at dusk, Zoe, Shawn, Celia, Meg, and Tia collapsed into the chairs on the front porch. Two bottles of champagne sat at the ready in a bucket filled with ice, and tea lights glowed from short, clear-glass candleholders on the end tables.

"What. A. Day," Shawn said, enunciating each word dramatically.

"No kidding." Meg leaned against the back of the chair and sighed. "I've never been so nervous in my life, not even on my first day in a professional kitchen."

Zoe rolled her eyes. "You had nothing to worry about." She looked over at Tia. "Tia and I had to deal with the Great Flood."

"I still have no idea how that happened," Shawn said. "I did a quick check of everything this morning and it was just fine." He shrugged. "But that's kind of how things work with plumbing. It's just fine until it suddenly isn't. Anyway, the plumber got everything fixed up and the flooring should be dried out before our first guest arrives tomorrow."

"That sounds so crazy," Meg said, her voice full of wonder. "Our first guest."

"I know," Zoe said. "It all happened so fast."

"Not fast," Celia said. "At the right time." She smiled serenely. "Everything happens at the right time, you just may not know it until later."

Tia watched them, feeling slightly out of place. She was the only person present who didn't hold an ownership stake in the resort. An easy camaraderie flowed between the others, but she'd only been working at the Inn for two months. Although her friendship was growing with Zoe, it was still in its infancy. Would she ever have the close relationships they seemed to have with each other?

"You're being awfully quiet," Celia said to Tia. "Did you have fun today?"

Tia smiled. "I did. And I think everyone else did too. I can't imagine a better grand opening." She laughed. "Well, without the flood."

"You were a big part of making this event successful." Zoe regarded her thoughtfully. "You know that right?"

"Eh. It's my job." Tia felt the heat rising into her cheeks, grateful that no one would be able to see it in the waning light.

"Your job was to help coordinate the event. I'm pretty sure there wasn't anything in your job description that included mopping up bathrooms—or my tears." Zoe scooted to the edge of the loveseat she shared with Shawn, the flickering candles casting shadows on her face. "If it hadn't been for you, I'd probably still be up there in that bathroom, bawling my eyes out."

Shawn reached out to rub Zoe's back, but didn't say anything.

"And you talked me down from the ledge too," Meg added. "You didn't have to do that."

Their praise hit Tia hard, and the emotions rising in her chest made it difficult to breathe. "Thank you. I'm happy to be here, working with all of you." She pasted a bright smile on her face. "And I'm so glad the grand opening was a success."

"We are too, honey." Celia reached an arm out toward her walker. "Now, who's ready for some celebration cake and champagne?"

Shawn leapt up before Celia could stand. "Sit, Grandma. I'll get the cake from the kitchen."

"And I'll pour the champagne." Meg removed a bottle from the ice bucket.

In all of the bustle, Tia almost didn't hear the little ping from her phone. She pulled it out of her small event purse and turned it on. It glowed brightly on the dark porch, revealing two missed calls from her mother.

She stuffed the phone back in her purse. Her mom could wait. This was a special night and she wasn't going to let her mom's overbearing negativity spoil it for her.

"Here you go, dear."

Tia looked up to see Celia holding out a bubbling glass of champagne.

When Shawn returned, his grandmother gave him one also. He raised his glass in the air. "To the Inn, and to sharing it with good friends and family."

"Cheers!" Everyone clinked their glasses together, creating a beautiful sound in one of the most perfect moments Tia had ever experienced.

12

SAMANTHA

Sam paced the living room of her one-bedroom apartment. The tenant below probably wouldn't appreciate the extra noise, but she needed to work off some of her nervous energy. It was the last day of August and she still hadn't heard back from any of the teaching jobs she'd applied for. At this rate, it was either time to find a new career or move to a different area. She had no desire to do either, but with only a few months of rent saved, she'd need to find something soon.

Tonight, though, she was determined not to let any of it bother her. Meg had fixed her up with her friend, Taylor, and he'd be there any minute to take her out on a date. Sam didn't have any illusions that Taylor would turn out to be the love of her life, but going out with him would get her family off her back. They seemed convinced that she was falling into depression and being out in public would reassure them she was fine. Besides, she deserved some fun, right?

The voice in the back of her head pushed its way through to the forefront of her thoughts: *Do I deserve it?* She'd broken Brant's heart. Did she really deserve to find happiness with someone else?

She hadn't meant to hurt him. He was her best friend, and she'd thought he was the love of her life. But after they were engaged and she couldn't muster up excitement over their wedding, she'd known something was wrong. The feelings she had for him were more brotherly than romantic. They'd broken up about a month ago and she still thought about him every day, although they hadn't talked since the breakup. Falling in love with your best friend was wonderful while it lasted, but devastating when it ended.

Getting back into the dating world wasn't a bad idea, but a blind date with her sister's ex-boss wouldn't have been her first choice. How often did that type of thing really work out? Besides, she'd seen Taylor a few times when Meg still worked at the Willa Bay Lodge, so it wasn't exactly a blind date. He was reasonably attractive and, per Meg, "a really great guy".

She looked down at the living room carpet, almost surprised that her repetitive pacing hadn't worn a path from the kitchen to the sliding glass door that led to the deck. A sound interrupted her thoughts and confused her for a second, until she realized what it was—the doorbell. She spun around and hurried to the front door. A quick glance out of the peephole confirmed that Taylor had arrived.

She opened the door and stepped back to give him the option to step inside or wait in the interior hallway of her apartment building. "Hi."

"Hi." He stuck out his hand. "I've seen you around, but I don't think we've ever formally met. I'm Taylor."

She laughed and accepted his handshake. "Well, I'm Samantha, but you can call me Sam. Nice to meet you."

"Nice to meet you too." He smiled widely at her, then chuckled nervously. "This feels a little awkward." He shifted his weight from one polished leather oxford to the other. He was taller than she'd remembered, with black spiky hair that came close to hitting the top of the door frame.

"Yeah. I know what you mean." Looking up at him, she was reminded of when she was a preteen and had pined over the boys in her older sisters' circles of friends. "Uh, I'll go get my purse and jacket, and then we can go."

"Sure." He leaned against the doorframe, making no move to enter her apartment.

She returned less than a minute later, wearing a pair of high heels that matched the red flowers on her sleeveless sundress. After she locked the door, they went out to the parking lot. The temperature earlier in the day had been the hottest all week, and the pavement still retained some of the heat, making the evening seem warmer than it actually was.

"I made a reservation at a new restaurant in Paddle Creek," he said. "Their chef has been getting a lot of good press and I'd like to check out his food. Does that work for you?"

She nodded. "I'm not too picky." Paddle Creek was about thirty minutes north of Willa Bay. Like her hometown, it was located on the Salish Sea, but Sam hadn't been there since she was a kid.

He turned on the radio to an easy listening station as soon as they got in the car, but didn't make much of an effort to chat with her. After she'd made a few attempts at small talk that were met with single-word responses, she focused on the passing scenery. The tulips the area was known for wouldn't be in bloom again until next spring, but there were plenty of scenic farms to admire along the way.

They arrived at the restaurant, located in a large, old house a few blocks from the water and pulled into one of the last spaces in the parking lot next door. As they walked along the path to the front door, Sam peered at the building.

"This house must have belonged to one of the original settlers in Paddle Creek," she said. "I love what they've done with the porch." In fact, she was almost hoping that their reservation would be delayed so she could check out the comfortable-looking loveseats outside the door and enjoy the warm evening breeze.

Taylor scanned the building and nodded appreciatively. "It is beautiful. I remember reading that it was built by a lumber baron around the turn of the century."

A well-dressed couple walked past them as they were observing the restaurant's exterior, and a flicker of concern made her pause a moment longer. Taylor had told her they'd be going out to dinner, so she'd opted for a long cotton sundress with a thin, knit sweater. Was this the type of place with a dress code?

He smiled at her. "Are you ready to go inside?"

She nodded, and they continued on down the path and up the steep stairs to the porch. When they entered the restaurant, Sam's eyes barely had time to adjust to the dim lighting before a hostess wearing a white blouse and black pencil skirt whisked her and Taylor away to a table covered in white linen, next to a window overlooking the garden. A narrow crystal vase containing a single rose surrounded by baby's breath completed the elegant ambience. The waiter came by immediately to fill their water glasses, saying he'd be back in a few minutes to take their order.

"This is nice," she whispered as she opened her menu. She looked around to see what the other patrons were wearing. Thank goodness she'd dressed up more than she usually would have for a date, but she still felt underdressed. This was one of the fanciest restaurants she'd ever been in, and it was more than a little intimidating. It was also very romantic for a first date, which didn't help her uneasiness.

Taylor surveyed the room. "It is nice. I hope the food is just as good." He looked at his menu, his finger tracing a line down the middle of each page as he read the descriptions. At the end of the final page, he clapped the menu shut and laid it on the table.

After they'd given the waiter their selections, they sat in awkward silence for a few minutes. Delectable aromas wafted through the air when the table next to them received their entrées, causing Sam's mouth to water. She took a long drink of water to keep her stomach from making a mortifying grumble in agreement with her mouth.

Taylor cleared his throat. "So, I hear you're a teacher?"

She nodded. "I'm a PE teacher at the high school." She frowned. "I mean, I *was* a PE teacher at the high school. There were some budget cuts and my contract wasn't renewed for the upcoming school year."

"Oh." He looked stricken. "I'm so sorry. That must have been rough. Have you been able to find anything else?"

"No." She played with the cloth napkin in her lap, running her fingers over the raised threads along the edge. "Nothing yet." So far, this wasn't going too well. Her mind raced, trying to think of something to say that would change the topic away from how badly she was currently failing in life to something more interesting. Asking him about his life seemed safe enough. "So, how long have you been a chef?"

"About ten years." He launched into an explanation of how he'd ended up in culinary school, his face lighting up as he described his experiences in some of the biggest restaurants on the West Coast.

"You love it, don't you?" She tilted her head to the side, studying his expression as she waited for him to respond. The way he talked about cooking was the same way she felt about teaching, especially educating kids about the importance of physical activity.

"I do." He beamed. "Growing up, I never saw myself becoming a chef, but it's the best job in the world. I love making people happy through the food I create for them and I love being the head chef at the Willa Bay Lodge. I feel so lucky to have found my dream job."

She smiled in agreement, feeling like they'd finally reached some common ground. "I get it. I feel the same way about what I do. To me, teaching students to become better versions of themselves is the best job in the world." In that instant, she knew that no matter what she decided to pursue for a future career, it needed to involve teaching in some form, whether that be through a coaching position or something else.

They talked about what they loved about their jobs until their orders came, at which point Taylor shut down in favor of digging into his beef bourguignon. Sam didn't mind though. Her own pan-seared salmon with avocado remoulade was excellent, and after their conversation about how important being a chef was to him, his single-minded focus didn't surprise her.

After he'd had a chance to get a good taste of

everything, Taylor finally looked up at her. "I'm so sorry. I just realized I was totally ignoring you." He grinned sheepishly. "I tend to hyperfocus when I'm eating something new. How is your meal? I promise I'll be a better date now that I've tried these dishes."

She took a sip of water, then grinned at him. "I didn't mind. I was enjoying my food too. You were right. This restaurant is excellent."

"What do you think about getting dessert?" he asked.

"Uh." She glanced around at the other diners. While she liked the restaurant, she was feeling increasingly self-conscious about what she was wearing. Her sundress was fine for most restaurants, but some of the women in this place were dressed to the nines.

He smiled. "It's a little stuffy in here, isn't it?"

She shot him a grateful look.

"What would you think about grabbing some ice cream down at the marina?" he suggested. "It's such a perfect evening for it."

"I'd like that," she said.

Their waiter brought them their check after they declined dessert. As Taylor pulled out his credit card and handed it to the waiter, he asked, "Would it be possible to speak with the chef before we leave? I'd like to pay my compliments. I'm a chef in Willa Bay and I thought this was a fantastic meal." He turned his attention to Sam. "Is that okay with you?"

"Of course."

"Certainly sir," the waiter said. "I'll go back to the kitchen and arrange for him to visit your table."

The chef came out and he and Taylor had a lively conversation for about five minutes, while Sam sat back and listened. Hearing them talk reminded her of how excited Meg got when she spoke about trying new recipes.

While Sam enjoyed cooking, she didn't get fired up about it like they did. When the two were done chatting and the other man had returned to the kitchen, Taylor stood.

"Thanks for letting us jabber on." He laughed self-consciously. "When chefs get to talking..."

"No problem." She pushed her chair back and looped her purse strap over her shoulder. "I didn't mind at all."

They walked the few blocks from the restaurant to a small marina, where a shack sat on the edge of the water. A long line of people snaked along the sidewalk in front of it.

They took their place in the queue and Sam eyed the list of flavors. "I think I'm going to go with the Northwest Blackberry."

"I was thinking the same thing," he said. "I like to try whatever's local when I go places."

"Are you originally from this area?" She knew he hadn't lived in Willa Bay for more than a few years, but she didn't know much about him other than that.

He shook his head. "Nope. I'm from Southern California, born and raised."

"Do you still have family there?" she asked, walking forward a few steps as the line moved.

"Three sisters, two older and one younger." His gaze trailed a boat puttering out of the slow water zone toward the breakwater.

"You must miss them."

"I do." His eyes took on a far-off look, then focused on her. "Are you close with your sisters? It must be nice to have them living in the same town as you."

"Yeah. We're pretty close." She lightly traced the sole of her right high-heeled shoe along the cement. "We don't always agree on everything, but we still hang out fairly often. My mom insists on family dinners at least once a month, although she'd prefer we got together even more frequently."

He stared at the ice cream shack while asking, "Do you and Meg get along? She seems like she'd be a fun sister."

Sam shrugged. "We do, especially since we're closer in age than I am with Libby. But we're very different too."

"Oh. Well, it must be nice to have her back home after she was gone for so long." He kept his gaze trained on the service counter. "We should be to the front soon."

"Yeah." She turned her head up to see his face better. He was a handsome guy, and Meg had been right about him being nice. Any woman would be happy to be out on a date with him. Unfortunately, no matter how much Sam tried to convince herself she should be attracted to him, there was no spark between them yet.

They got their ice cream and walked along the dock, checking out all of the different types of boats moored there.

"Meg's boyfriend lives on a boat, right?" he asked.

She scanned the marina, then pointed to a sailboat a few docks away. "Yeah, something similar to that sailboat."

"Ah." He looked down at his dessert and took a huge bite. "Do you think she's serious about him?" he mumbled.

Sam stopped abruptly. Now that she was no longer moving, the sway of the dock was much more apparent. "You know, I don't really know. They've been together for a few months, but I've only met him once. I only know what his boat looks like because Meg pointed it out to me when we were down at the Willa Bay Marina." She cocked her head to the side. "Why do you ask?"

"Oh, no reason," he said quickly, stuffing the rest of his cone in his mouth.

"You're not interested in my sister, are you?" It seemed

like a weird thing to ask on a first date, but the words spilled out before she could censor them.

He choked slightly and swallowed. "Like romantically?" He cleared his throat, avoiding her eyes.

"Yeah." She peered at him. "Are you?" And if he was interested in Meg, why had he agreed to go out on a date with her younger sister?

"No, of course not. We're just friends." He started walking again, this time toward the ramp leading off the docks.

She jogged to keep up with him. When they reached the top of the ramp, she tapped him on the shoulder. "Are you sure?"

"Sure of what?" he asked, nonchalant.

"That you don't have a thing for Meg." She stared at him.

He sighed, then said in an irritated voice, "There's nothing going on between Meg and me."

Sam noticed he'd sidestepped her question, but she wasn't going to press the matter further. One thing was for sure though—Taylor had feelings for her sister, whether he knew it or not. The walk back to the restaurant parking lot seemed to take twice as long in silence as it had when they'd chatted amicably on the way to the marina.

On the ride home she again made an effort to entice him into conversation, and this time she was successful. As they chatted, the walls Taylor had erected earlier seemed to melt away. When he reached her apartment complex, he dropped her off at the front of her unit, and they said friendly goodbyes before she got out of the car and walked herself to her door.

Up until she'd asked him about Meg, she'd had a good time, so this hadn't been the worst date ever. However, it was safe to say there wouldn't be a second one, as he obviously had feelings for her sister.

Still, her family had been right. Going out with Taylor had made her realize that she needed to have more fun, and that breaking up with Brant hadn't been the end to her social life. She and Taylor hadn't been a match made in heaven, but her time would come. Until then, she had plenty of time to figure out the other aspects of her life.

13

"You seem like you've been feeling a little down lately." Debbie's husband Peter set his fork on his empty plate and peered at her from his customary seat across from her at the dining room table. "Is there something going on?"

Debbie pushed strands of noodles around her plate, twirling them into intricate patterns and piles. A thick lump had formed in her throat, making it impossible to eat. "I've been kind of out of sorts since finding out about Diana's death last month." It had started well before that, to be truthful, but the shock of discovering her friend had died brought her sense of unrest to the forefront.

"I'm sorry, honey. I know her death hit you hard. Is there anything I can do to help?"

She shrugged and met his eyes, which were full of kind sympathy as he regarded her. She swallowed hard, then said, "I don't know. I'm not used to feeling like this— like I'm not in control of my own life."

He frowned, deep furrows lining his forehead.

"Nobody has complete control over what happens to them." He got up from his chair and moved closer to her, rubbing his hand lightly across her back. His touch was warm and comforting, but at the same time threatened to break through her outward composure. "Is it only your friend's death, or is there something more?"

She didn't know how to answer him. It was Diana's death, compounded by the nagging feeling that she wasn't living her own life to the fullest. After existing in a constant state of fear that the cancer was going to steal dozens of years from her life, the scans last spring had come back clean. At that point, she'd started to breathe easier, finally allowing herself to believe that she had a future. Thinking about what lay ahead had come with its own issues.

For the last few decades, she'd happily embraced her role as a mother, and later, a business owner. The two years following her cancer diagnosis had been the first time in a while that she'd stepped off of the crazy merry-go-round of life and experienced a significant amount of downtime. Since then, she'd been taking stock of what was truly important to her. Those ruminations had screeched to a halt when Libby's financial situation changed and she'd needed their catering company to take on more jobs.

Debbie looked up at her husband of thirty-nine years, hope leaping to the surface. "Can we take a trip to Italy?" she asked impulsively. "Maybe next spring, for our fortieth anniversary? I hear the countryside is gorgeous in the spring."

He leaned back in his chair to process her request. When he finally spoke, the words came out slowly, as though he were pushing them through a vat of molasses. "I don't know if I can get the time off for an international vacation. Things have been hectic lately at work." He studied her face intently and she knew he didn't want to disappoint her. Still, it was the same thing he'd told every time she asked.

She stared at him, biting her lower lip. Would his answer ever change? "Things are always crazy at your work. We haven't taken a long vacation in years." Her eyes filled with tears. "Please, Peter. This is important to me."

He softened, pulling her close and kissing her temple. She melted against him, feeling so emotionally fragile that she might collapse into a puddle of tears at any minute. Seeing the sights of Italy had long been a dream of hers, but now it had become a symbol for everything she wanted to do with the time she had left on earth.

"I'll see what I can do," he whispered into her hair. He held her close for a few minutes.

When she felt stronger, she sniffled, and sat up. "I'm sorry," she said in a low voice. "I don't know what's wrong with me. I do want to take a nice vacation with you, but I know I sound crazy." Here she was, a mature woman in her early sixties, and she was acting like a teenager who hadn't received the car she'd begged for.

"You don't sound crazy." He cupped her chin and gently kissed her lips. "I don't know what's going on either, but we'll work it out together. I want you to be happy. You know that, right?"

She hiccupped a little as she tried to stem the flow of tears, whispering, "I know." She dabbed at her eyes with her unused table napkin. "But what if even I don't know what I want?"

He met her gaze, staring deeply into her eyes as he spoke. "I think you need to figure out what makes you happy and go for it. You've spent so many years of your life trying to make other people happy. You deserve a chance to find that happiness for yourself, even if it means letting other people down." He pushed his chair back and reached for her hands, squeezing them between his own in a gesture that always comforted her.

Libby. Deep down, Debbie knew she had to tell Libby that she couldn't continue working so many hours in the catering kitchen. The extra workload was causing her too much stress. But who could she trust to help? She'd spent so many years building the business's reputation, and although she knew Libby could manage the company's day-to-day operations, she'd need consistent help with the actual catering jobs. Unfortunately, Debbie didn't know anyone who fit the bill *and* was available.

She let out a slow, deep exhale, hoping it would give her much-needed clarity. "Libby needs the money from the catering business. She's been a nervous wreck since Gabe was officially laid off last week. Now isn't the right time to tell her I don't want to work so much. She needs me."

"Could Samantha help out more with the business?" Peter asked, immediately going into solve-it mode.

Debbie shook her head. "She can work for us on the weekends, but she's got her teaching job during the week." She frowned. Something was going on with her youngest daughter, but Debbie didn't know what. It could just be residual sadness from the breakup with Brant, but Debbie sensed there were other issues in play as well.

Peter sighed. "I'm sure there's something that can be done to keep the catering company running but still allow you more freedom to pursue your own interests." He returned to his seat and drained the contents of his water glass. "I'll ask for two weeks off in the spring so we can take that trip, but it's not going to solve all of your problems. Something has to give."

Debbie's spirits lifted. It was a longshot for him to get the time off of work, but at least now he was seriously considering the trip. If only the other problems nipping at her could be fixed by a simple request.

"I know. I'll work on a plan for the business." She offered him a small smile to let him know she was feeling better.

He smiled back at her, picked up his empty plate and nodded to hers. "Are you done? You've barely eaten a thing."

He was right. She glanced at the mound of linguine with clam sauce congealing on her dinner plate. It was virtually untouched, but she felt no desire to eat. "I think I'll save it for later."

He took it from her, sealed it with plastic wrap, and placed it in the refrigerator. She rose from the table too, and rinsed off dishes accumulating in the sink before filling the dishwasher. The familiarity of the mundane chore gave her a brief respite from her internal conflict. Peter excused himself to his den to pay bills, and she collapsed in her favorite recliner.

A trip to look forward to was a start, but she needed something more. Debbie's brow furrowed as she picked up her knitting supplies from the basket on the floor beside her. What *would* make her happy? Her kids and grandkids did, for sure, but she needed to find something of her own as well, something that would give her life meaning.

She thought while her knitting needles clicked together furiously, adding rows on to the winter hat she'd started for her granddaughter, Kaya. As the hat grew, so did a flurry of ideas. She smiled. Somehow, she'd solve her dilemma with the catering company, and then she'd be free to focus on the project taking shape in her mind.

14

Taylor

Taylor squeezed his eyes shut more tightly as the plane's wheels bounced a few times on the runway, only opening them when it slowed to a sedate roll across the tarmac. Every time he flew, he thought his fear of flying would decrease. So far, that hadn't happened. It wasn't that he had a fear of heights—he was perfectly fine climbing the face of a mountain. He had an irrational fear the plane would suddenly fall out of the sky.

"You're not a fan of flying, are you?" asked the white-haired woman next to him. She smiled kindly and the tightness in his chest decreased.

He took a deep breath and chuckled a little. "No, not really. I try to avoid it whenever possible." He glanced out the window. Heat radiated off of the blacktop as the baggage handlers worked swiftly to unload the baggage from the plane's belly. He looked back at his seatmate. "I am glad to be home though."

"Oh? Do you live here?"

"No, I actually live in Washington now, but I grew up in this area." He stretched out his legs as much as possible. When he had to fly, he always tried to get a seat in the exit row for the extra leg room, but it hadn't been available on this flight. Normally, he preferred to drive the 1300 miles between Willa Bay and San Diego, but it was the busy season at the Lodge, and he'd been lucky just to get Labor Day weekend off to attend his sister's wedding.

"Ah. I see." She turned slightly in her seat and pointed at a family a few rows down. "My daughter, son-in-law, and grandkids are here on vacation. We're looking forward to seeing the zoo."

He nodded. "You'll enjoy it. I have good memories of going there for a class field trip in elementary school." The people seated in front of them moved into the aisle and grabbed their bags, so both Taylor and the woman stood. He removed his backpack from the overhead compartment, then pulled her carry-on out as well.

"Thank you." She beamed as he set the hard plastic case in front of her. "I hope you enjoy your time at home."

"Thanks. I hope you and your family have a wonderful vacation. It's supposed to be beautiful this week." He turned around and waited patiently as a man in front of him wrestled an overstuffed suitcase free from the bins. Finally, it was their turn to deplane.

Heat blasted through the walls of the jet bridge, making him wish he'd worn shorts for the trip. He was grateful for the air-conditioned interior of the airport, however, as he followed the overhead signs to baggage claim. When he stepped out of the secure area, a tall woman with long black hair parted on the side came out of nowhere and threw her arms around him.

The force of her assault and the weight of his backpack knocked him about a half-step backward. After recovering from the surprise, he hugged his younger sister tightly, filling with a sense of happiness and home. "Suzy-Q! What are you doing here? I thought Mom and Dad were going to wait for me outside." He released her and held her at arm's length.

Susanna laughed. "Nope, the whole family's here. Well, minus Diana. She had some primping to do before her bachelorette party tonight."

He looked past her and saw his parents and his sister, Cammie, along with Cammie's young boys, Jason and Andrew. "Wow. You weren't kidding. This is quite a homecoming."

"We couldn't do anything less for the prodigal son," Susanna quipped. "You finally decided to deign us with your presence, so we're not going to let any of your time at home go to waste."

He mock-scowled at her. She returned the look, then giggled just like she used to do when they were kids.

His dad stepped up and clapped him on the back. "Good to see you, Taylor," he said gruffly.

"We've missed you." Tears welled in his mother's eyes, sending tendrils of guilt winding their way through his veins.

"I came home last Christmas," he protested. "It's not like I've been gone for years." He looked over at Cammie's sons, who were tugging at their mother's hands, bouncing in place as they waited their turn to say hi to him. They'd both grown so much in the last nine months. He'd talked to them over video calls, but it hadn't been the same as seeing them in person.

"It might as well be." His mother pulled him into her arms like he was a small child and not a grown man who towered over her petite frame.

When their mother was done greeting Taylor,

Cammie let her sons loose. They ran to him and hugged his legs in the vise grip perfected by small children and monkeys.

Taylor grinned at Cammie. "I think they missed me."

She smiled. "They've talked about little else for the last week than you coming home. Don't tell Diana, but I'm pretty sure your visit is way more important to them than her wedding."

Four-year-old Andy looked up at him and stuck out his tongue. "Ew, weddings."

All of the adults laughed, and Andy wrinkled his nose indignantly. Taylor picked up little Jason, who weighed less than his backpack, as the baggage carousel started its rotation. He set him next to Cammie and Andy, a safe distance away from where passengers were dragging their luggage off the conveyor belt.

Taylor spotted his navy-blue, full-size suitcase and grabbed it, extending the handle as he rejoined his family.

Susanna raised an eyebrow. "Aren't you only here for a few days? You must pack more than any woman I've ever known."

"No." He shot her an icy death glare that made her smirk. "My dress suit wouldn't fit in any of my other suitcases without getting wrinkled. Everything else could have fit in my carry-on." He prided himself on his ability to pack efficiently, and although he knew she was teasing, he felt oddly defensive about it.

Although he had made friends in Willa Bay, being home with his family was completely different. They knew all of his little quirks, and exactly how to needle him. In Willa Bay, he'd only developed that type of friendship with one person—Meg. Spending countless hours together in the kitchen had given them an easy familiarity. Even so, the time they'd spent together recently made him realize how little they still knew about each other.

He looked at his watch. "Is anyone else hungry? The only thing they gave us on the flight was a bag of stale crackers."

Cammie grinned. "Oh, little brother, you haven't changed a bit. Always thinking about food, just like when you were a teenager." She eyed her boys ruefully. "I'm not looking forward to our grocery bills when these two get a little older."

"Dad and I were thinking we'd take you out to dinner tonight." His mom peered up at him. "Is that okay? I still feel weird cooking for a professional chef."

They'd had this conversation too many times over the years. He shook his head. "Mom, you have nothing to worry about. I love your cooking." She didn't look convinced. He looked at his sisters. "Are you going to be joining us at the restaurant?"

Cammie shook her head. "Nope. We're going to meet up with the rest of the girls for Diana's bachelorette party. I'm going to stop by the house and drop the boys off with Darren first, but they didn't want to miss out on seeing their Uncle Taylor tonight. I'll see you tomorrow at the wedding, okay?"

He nodded.

Susanna put her hand on his back. "See you later. We need to catch up. I want to hear all about your life up in Seattle."

There wasn't anything exciting to tell her about his life, but she'd never believe that. "Sure. Have fun tonight."

Susanna winked at him. "Oh, we will." She took Andy's hand and followed Cammie and Jason over to the elevator leading to the parking garage.

His dad cleared his throat. "Do you have everything?"

Taylor pushed his massive suitcase out in front of him and grinned. "I can't imagine what I could have forgotten."

They left the airport and stopped at Chang's, his favorite Chinese restaurant, a few miles away from his parents' house. When he slid into the booth across from his parents, noting the familiar cracks in the red vinyl seat, nostalgia hit. They'd come here for every one of his birthdays when he was a kid, and his parents brought him here every time he came home to visit. Like always, his mom started grilling him about his life in Willa Bay as soon as they'd ordered their food.

"How are things going at work?" she asked. She poured herself a cup of jasmine tea and blew on the surface, sending little ripples across the amber liquid.

The waitress came by to drop off their appetizer, and while she was rearranging their place settings to fit the massive pupu platter she was about to set on the table, Taylor finished off the last drop of tea in his own cup. He refilled it, then put it down to cool. "Things are going well. I still love my job." A vision of his neat, orderly kitchen at the Lodge came to mind. When he'd originally requested vacation days for Diana's wedding, Meg had still been his second-in-command. His new sous-chef wasn't quite up to the task of taking over for a few nights, so although Meg was no longer an employee at the Lodge, the Lodge's owner, George Camden, had allowed Meg to step in for the long weekend. Meg had been concerned about coming back after her disagreement with George's daughter, Lara, but she'd reluctantly agreed to fill in for Taylor so he could attend the wedding.

Taylor frowned. He'd hated to put Meg in such an awkward position, and hoped she hadn't felt obligated to help him because he'd assisted her with the barn. Unfortunately, he was short on options and they couldn't close the kitchen on Labor Day weekend. Lara didn't work on the weekends, so with any luck, everything would go smoothly for Meg.

"Is everything okay?" His mom set her fork down and peered at him. "You seem troubled."

His father stuffed half an egg roll in his mouth and looked at the table, avoiding the conversation. Taylor could count on his hand the number of times he and his father had talked about serious subjects, and he knew he could count on his dad to be there for him when needed, but Taylor also knew the man did not like awkward situations.

Taylor faced his mom. "No, not at all." His stomach twisted at the denial. "I'm just a bit worried because I left the restaurant in the hands of my former sous-chef and things were a little weird when she left the Lodge." He relayed to them the whole tale of the renovations at the Inn at Willa Bay and Meg's subsequent departure from the Lodge.

His father raised an eyebrow. "Wow. It seems like a lot has happened since the last time you were here."

Taylor paused for a moment. He spoke to his family fairly often. Had he not told them about all of this? He'd known that leaving the Lodge was the right choice for Meg, but it hadn't been an easy transition for him. He swallowed a wave of uneasiness that had formed in the back of his throat and washed it down with a slug of lukewarm tea.

"It sounds like you miss having Meg in the kitchen," his mother said. "You used to talk about her all the time, but you stopped sometime over the summer. I always wondered why, but I didn't want to pry."

He wasn't sure how to respond to that, so he followed his father's lead on avoidance tactics, and stuck his fork into a slice of barbecued pork. He dipped the marinated meat into Chinese hot mustard, followed by a generous coating of sesame seeds. Even after years working in some of the best restaurants on the West Coast, he'd yet to find better Chinese food than Chang's.

"Taylor?" His mother prompted. "Why didn't you tell us that Meg had left?" She glanced at his father, who immediately grabbed the other half of his egg roll. She rolled her eyes and turned her focus back on her son.

Taylor finished chewing the pork, then shrugged. "I don't know. It must have slipped my mind." He put his hands flat on the table and pushed himself out of the booth. "I'm going to visit the men's room before our dinner arrives."

His mom looked like she wanted to say something, but a warning glance from his dad stopped her.

The food had arrived by the time Taylor returned. Steaming platters of cashew chicken, broccoli beef, pork fried rice, and chicken chow mein had been crammed onto the tabletop, interspersed between their place settings and appetizer dishes.

"This looks great." Taylor helped himself to as much as he could fit on his plate and started eating.

The rest of their meal and evening together were uneventful, and, thankfully, his mother didn't mention Meg again.

~

The next morning, Taylor slept in until ten o'clock, and was awakened by the sound of little footsteps pounding down the hallway outside his room like a herd of tiny elephants.

"Boys," Cammie said in a mock-whisper that could

clearly be heard through the closed guestroom door. "Uncle Taylor is still sleeping." She said in an even louder voice that held a hint of humor, "I bet he could use a wakeup visit from two little boys though."

Not thirty seconds later, Jason and Andy flung open the door. Taylor pretended to be asleep under the covers and readied himself for the onslaught.

The boys pounced on his still form, and he surprised them by sitting up and trapping them in his arms. "Gotcha."

They shrieked, then broke out into a fit of giggles. Their laughter was so infectious that Taylor couldn't help joining in. He released them after a minute of letting them struggle playfully against his grip, then sent them off to find their mother, took a quick shower, and dressed.

As soon as he'd finished, he ventured down the hall and found the boys and his parents eating a big pancake breakfast, complete with scrambled eggs, bacon, and strawberries.

"What happened to Cammie?" he asked as he filled a cup with coffee. He sat down at the table in front of an empty plate.

"All of the women in the wedding party have appointments at the hair salon this morning," his mom said. "Cammie drew the short stick and had to take the earliest one. Afterward, she's going to help get things ready down at the church. Darren is working today, so we've got the kids. Well, your father has the kids. I've got to head out soon too." She held out the plate of bacon. "Take as much as you'd like. I made plenty."

"Thanks." He grinned at the kids. "Sounds like you and Grandpa and I are going to have some fun today."

They both nodded enthusiastically, and Taylor's spirits lifted. He didn't know Diana's fiancé well, and hadn't been upset to not be one of the groomsmen, but he'd wondered what he was going to do all day before the wedding began. Spending the day with the boys would be fun and a welcome change from the hectic pace of his job in the Lodge's kitchen.

A few hours with the boys dispelled any notions he had about having a relaxing day. By the time they'd cleaned the maple syrup off the kids, run around in the yard with them for a few hours, scrubbed off mud from playing in a puddle, brokered more than a few peace treaties when fights broke out, and got them down for a nap, Taylor was ready for a nap of his own.

"It's not as easy as it looks, huh?" His dad shot him a sympathetic look from his blue leather recliner. "I usually need about a week of rest after they spend a night here."

Taylor laughed as he eased his aching muscles into the matching recliner. "I don't know how Cammie and Darren do it."

"Practice." His dad grinned. "You have to work into it."

"Were we this much work?" Taylor leaned back and kicked out the footrest. "I don't remember ever having that much energy."

His dad chortled. "There were four of you, and every one of you were just as energetic as Cammie's boys. Your mom and I used to collapse into bed every night and wonder how we were going to do it all again the next day." He smiled, and a far-off look came over his face, as if reliving those days.

"We were that bad?" Taylor asked.

His dad sat upright, pushing the footrest in. Suddenly serious, he looked straight at his son. "I wouldn't change a minute of it." He ran his hand through his thinning brown hair and cleared his throat.

Taylor stilled, wondering what his dad was going to

say to him. "Dad? Is everything okay with your heart?" His father had experienced some chest pain the year before, but after a full battery of tests, the doctors had proclaimed him fit as a fiddle. Taylor had wanted to come out to see him when it happened, but his father had protested, saying it was unnecessary. His parents told him everything was fine since then, but had that been true?

His father sighed and Taylor's own heart seemed to stop. "Dad. What is it?" Usually calm in a crisis, Taylor barely recognized his own voice as the pitch rose with his growing panic.

"Shh." His dad cast a furtive glance at the room off the hall where they'd put Jason and Andy down to nap. "If you wake them up, they'll be crabby tonight and we'll take the blame."

Taylor sighed in exasperation, but spoke at lower level. "Dad. What aren't you telling me?"

His dad shook his head and stared at his hands in his lap, then locked eyes with Taylor. "There's nothing wrong with me. Your mom is worried about you." He expelled his breath sharply. "I'm worried about you."

His father's admission hit Taylor harder than the bad news he'd steeled himself against.

"I'm fine. I told you that last night. Everything's going great at work."

"Yes, I know. At work. We know you love your job at the Lodge." His father stared at the ceiling and then back at him. "But what about outside of work? Do you have friends? People you can talk to? You always had these huge groups of friends when you were growing up. Now you barely talk about anyone in Willa Bay. Your mom and I thought maybe this Meg girl was special to you, but then you stopped talking about her too."

"I have friends," he blurted out.

"But are you happy there?" His dad stood and paced around the living room, obviously uncomfortable discussing personal matters with his son. "We need to know if you're happy."

"I like living in Willa Bay." The question rang in his ears though. Was he happy? Last spring, he would have had no problem answering that question with a resounding *yes*. Now, it wasn't so easy. He missed having Meg in the kitchen with him every day—missed seeing her. Everything had changed when she'd left, and he'd spent the last couple of months floating along. He'd tried to fight his feelings for her, but he couldn't shake them—a fact that hadn't escaped Sam's attention on their date. If Sam saw it, did everyone else?

"Did something happen with Meg?" his dad asked.

"No!" Taylor got up too, pacing the opposite side of the room from his dad. "Nothing happened with her. We're just friends."

His dad stopped. "But you want to be more than friends."

Was he really having this conversation with his dad? It wouldn't have surprised him if his mom had confronted him about Meg, but his dad had never been the touchy-feely type.

"Maybe," Taylor admitted. "At one point. But she's dating someone and seems happy with him. She's not interested in me."

His dad crossed the room and grabbed Taylor's arms. Taylor looked up at him—a rarity for someone who was over six feet tall—and froze at the gravity on his father's face. This whole interaction was like something out of the Twilight Zone.

"If she's important to you, tell her how you really feel. And if that doesn't work, move on." He studied Taylor.

"Life is too short to be unhappy. I know your career is important to you, but I want you to know you're always welcome here if you want to look for another job a little closer to home. We'd all love to have you around more."

He pulled Taylor to him, hugging him fiercely. When they parted, Taylor could have sworn there were tears in his father's eyes.

"Thanks, Dad." From down the hall came the sound of a minor squabble and Taylor sighed. "Looks like we're in trouble."

His dad laughed. "Don't worry. I've got a secret weapon." He walked into the kitchen and returned with a bag of Hershey's Kisses.

Taylor raised an eyebrow. "Candy?"

"If I bribe them enough, they'll be as good as gold during the ceremony." He winked at Taylor. "Just don't tell your mom or Cammie."

Taylor laughed, feeling closer to his dad than he had for a long time. "My lips are sealed."

Taylor didn't have much time to dwell on his father's advice in the next few hours, which flew by as they got the boys a snack, dressed up in their wedding finery, and drove to the church located a few towns away. Waiting for the ceremony to start, however, was a different matter.

Seeing his family pull together to make Diana's wedding a success reminded him of how much he'd missed since he'd left town. His nephews were growing up so fast, and soon Diana would probably have children too. He wouldn't be a part of any of that.

Was his job at the Lodge worth the sacrifice? He loved having his own kitchen, and loved planning the menu and managing the restaurant. It was everything he'd always aspired to do. If he left, there was no guarantee that he'd ever find anything like it again. And although he hadn't given his parents a full run-down on his life in Willa Bay, he did have friends. He had a few buddies in Seattle that he saw once in a while, and through working at the Lodge together, he'd become friends with Cassie, Zoe, and Meg.

Meg. His father's advice to tell her how he felt wouldn't work because she was happy with Theo. So, where did that leave him? He couldn't keep torturing himself by being friends with her while he had feelings for her. Either he had to somehow forget about his attraction to her, or he had to leave town.

His eyes blurred with tears as he watched Diana walk down the aisle. Her smile was so brilliant that there was no doubt of her love for her husband-to-be, and from the look on the groom's face, the feeling was mutual. Would he ever get the chance to be that happy in love?

He swiped at his face with his fingers before his parents, seated next to him, could see him crying. Of course, they would probably be written off as happy tears, but he knew the truth. He smiled as his sister and her new husband walked back down the aisle, hand-in-hand. When they had reached the back of the church, the wedding party followed and everyone else filed out after them.

Taylor went through the receiving line to congratulate the bride and groom. He gave his sister a hug. "You look beautiful," he told her. To her husband, he said, "Welcome to the family," and shook his hand.

He meant it. Being back home had given him space to think and finalize his decision to leave Willa Bay. Now, he was looking forward to getting to know Diana's husband and spending more time with his whole family.

Later, Susanna joined Taylor for a pre-dinner drink. She sipped her Chardonnay and gazed over at the newlyweds. "They look happy, don't they? Her wistful tone caught Taylor's attention.

He smiled at her. "They do."

"Do you think we'll ever find our perfect matches?" she asked, echoing his thoughts from earlier.

"Probably not." He smirked at her, hoping to lighten the mood. "It would take a very special someone to fall in love with you."

"Taylor!" She slugged him on the arm. "That's not very nice."

"Okay, okay," he grumbled, rubbing the spot she'd hit. "I'm sure you'll find someone soon. I, on the other hand, will have to be content to be the doting uncle."

"I'm sure that's not true." She frowned at him. "What about that friend of yours you're always talking about? Meg?"

"She has a boyfriend. I'm not going to get into the middle of that."

"But you do have feelings for her?" She peered at him. "If you do, you should tell her."

It was like everyone was conspiring to fix him up with Meg. His phone rang before he could come up with a witty retort. He removed it from his pocket and checked the caller ID. It was the Lodge.

Why would someone be calling him from the Lodge while he was on vacation? Surely Meg and the rest of the staff could handle any issues that arose.

He answered. "Hello?"

"Taylor, this George Camden." His boss sounded weary. "I'm afraid I have some bad news."

He gripped his phone tighter. "What is it?"

George sighed, his breath coming out in a short puff that echoed over the phone line. "There's been a fire in the

Lodge's kitchen. The firemen are still working on putting it out."

Blood pounded in Taylor's ears. A fire? They were in the middle of the dinner rush. Meg! His chest constricted. "Is everyone okay?"

George sighed again. "There weren't any serious injuries, but Meg's been taken to the hospital to get checked out. She got everyone else out of there immediately, but inhaled a bit of smoke when she tried to put out the flames with the extinguisher."

Time stood still as Taylor's mind raced. Meg was hurt. "I'll be home on the next flight."

15

Meg

"You had all of us so worried." Libby hovered over Meg's hospital bed. "Next time, don't try to be a hero. Let the firemen do their job." Despite Libby's chiding, lines of fear etched her face and her voice trembled.

Meg gave her sister a weak smile. "I hope there isn't a next time." Like anyone who spent their days in a restaurant kitchen, she'd experienced her share of minor flare-ups, but nothing like the fire at the Lodge. She shivered despite the crisp white sheet and cotton blanket pulled up over her chest.

"Are you cold?" Libby immediately went into mom mode. "I can ask the nurse for another blanket." She glared at the ceiling vent which was puffing chilled air into the room. "I don't know why they have to make these rooms so frigid."

Meg had to grin at her sister's indignation, but in truth, it felt good to have someone so concerned for her well-being. "I'm fine. Stop worrying." Between her co-workers, the firemen, and the rest of her family's visit earlier, she'd already had enough coddling to last her a lifetime.

Libby shook her head, but sat down in a plastic chair next to Meg. "You could have been killed. I don't know what you were thinking."

Well, that makes two of us. Memories of the fire were stamped into her brain like a film reel, spinning repeatedly for the last few hours.

When she'd seen the flames shooting out of the deep fryer, she'd dropped what she was doing and grabbed a fire extinguisher. Lara was standing nearby, paralyzed, a mesh oil-skimmer dangling uselessly in her limp hand.

Meg had shouted for Lara to move out of the way, but she hadn't budged. The new sous-chef, Brandon, had grabbed Lara and guided her away from danger while Meg aimed the fire extinguisher at the fryer. She'd yelled at everyone to get out and call the fire department while she continued spraying foam at the growing flames. Her efforts did little to stop the fire's progression, and she'd watched helplessly as the walls behind the fryer blackened.

When the firemen arrived, they'd pried the extinguisher out of her hands and rushed her out of the kitchen and into a waiting ambulance. It had all been such a blur. Meg's breath came out in a shudder.

"Are you okay?" Libby's voice cut through the dark memory.

"Yeah. Just thinking about the fire." Meg pulled the covers up to her neck. Luckily, no one had been seriously injured. The damage hadn't extended to the main part of the Lodge, but the restaurant would be closed for a while.

Taylor would be horrified when he saw the current state of his beloved kitchen.

Ugh. He was out-of-state at his sister's wedding, and Meg hated that this would ruin his vacation time with his family. She'd tried so hard to keep the flames down, but even the large fire extinguisher had been no match for them. If only Lara had said something as soon as things got out of control, maybe the result would have been different. Or if Meg had been out in the kitchen instead of in Taylor's office making sure everything was set for the dinner service that evening, maybe she would have been able to prevent Lara's mistake.

She closed her eyes. All the maybes in the world weren't going to make the damage to the Lodge's kitchen disappear. Someone knocked on the open door and both Meg and Libby turned to look.

"Are you alright?" Theo asked. "Zoe called to let me know about the fire."

The fact that he'd come to the hospital reassured Meg that he cared about her. Even though neither of them had wanted anything serious when they'd started dating, they'd been together long enough that she was starting to want more from a relationship. Up until now though, she'd wondered if his feelings for her were purely superficial.

She smiled warmly at him. "I'm okay. I inhaled a bit of smoke, so they wanted to keep me here overnight for observation. But I'm basically fine."

Libby stood and assessed Theo, then leaned down to press her cheek to Meg's in an awkward, hospital-bed hug. "I'm going to head out, but call me if you need anything."

"I will. Thanks, Libby."

Libby left and Theo sat down in the chair she'd just vacated. "What happened?" he asked. "All Zoe said was that there was a fire and you were in the hospital. I was so worried."

"The deep fryer caught fire and part of the kitchen burned. I tried to put it out, but it wasn't enough."

"That sounds awful." He kissed her cheek and squeezed her left hand.

"It was." She gazed into space, reliving it once more. She knew she hadn't been the one in the wrong. Lara had been the one to start the fire with her ill-conceived plan to fry donuts without knowing what she was doing. However, that fact, much like the useless fire extinguisher, did little to quell the flames of guilt that continued to consume her. The kitchen had been Meg's responsibility.

"Hey," he said so brightly that she jerked to attention. "I have something to tell you."

She pushed herself upright and reached back to pile up some pillows as a backrest. "What is it?"

"I'm heading up to the San Juan Islands next weekend." He beamed at her. "And I was hoping you'd come with me."

She stared at him. "You mean for the weekend?" The Inn had just opened. There was no way she could get away for a few days.

"No." He shook his head and looked at her like she was being obtuse on purpose. "I've decided to explore the islands up there before winter comes."

"So, you're talking about a few months." She burrowed the back of her head into the pillows to think. Theo was asking her to leave Willa Bay—leave her friends, family, and the Inn for months.

"Yeah." He shrugged. "We'd be back by Christmas though."

"If I leave now," she said slowly, "Shawn and Zoe will want to push back the timeframe for renovating the barn."

He shot an exasperated look at the ceiling then focused on her. "Are you still stuck on that? I thought you'd change your mind after the Inn opened. Aren't you busy enough with the Inn?"

She gaped at him like a big-mouth bass, about to be filleted. Did he not understand how important having her own restaurant was to her? Had he taken all of their conversations so lightly that he'd failed to realize that?

"Yeah," she said in a level voice. "I want to renovate the barn. I know I can make it into something special."

He leaned back in the chair. "Okay. I hadn't realized you still wanted to do that." He was quiet for a moment.

In the stillness, Meg caught sight of a man's figure paused in the hallway outside of her room. He stood as still as a statue, his hands wrapped around a large bouquet of flowers. For a moment, she thought it was Taylor. When he called out to someone further down the hall, she realized she'd been mistaken.

Theo spoke, but she couldn't concentrate enough to process what he was saying. After the terrifying evening she'd had, she'd wanted it to be Taylor in the hallway – wanted the comfort of his presence. At the same time, she was glad it hadn't been. The restaurant fire had happened on her watch, and she wasn't sure if he'd blame her for it.

"Meg? Did you hear what I said?" Theo asked.

She glanced at the empty doorway again, then smiled apologetically. "No, sorry. I was a little lost in thought."

"I was saying that you could join me for a month or so, then come back here and work on your project." He flashed her the smile that usually made her heart drop.

This time though, it gave her pause. He wasn't taking her aspirations to fix up the barn seriously. Was he right? Was she crazy to think that she could rebuild that old, decrepit barn?

"So, what do you think?" he asked. "Do you want to come sail the islands with me?"

"I think I need to rest now." She nestled further into the pillows until she was in a fully reclined position. "This has been a really long day."

He nodded and kissed her forehead. "I understand. Let me know as soon as you can, though, about the trip. I'm planning on leaving in a few days."

"I will," she promised.

He walked jauntily out of the room with his hands in pockets, a man without a care in the world. She watched him until he disappeared into a group of nurses, then closed her eyes. Theo's proposition was enticing—a chance to escape everything and just enjoy being free to explore the waterways of the Salish Sea.

Doubts clouded Meg's mind, jumbling her thoughts. She was willing to bet that a huge portion of the population would accept Theo's offer in a heartbeat. Sailing amidst the breathtaking beauty of the San Juan Islands was an opportunity of a lifetime. But what if she and Theo couldn't get along in the confines of a small sailboat?

On the other hand, if she stayed in Willa Bay, was her goal to renovate the barn and build an award-winning restaurant nothing more than a pipe dream? Weariness overcame her and she drifted into a deep sleep that lasted until morning, only awakening for a few minutes at a time when the nurses came in to check her vitals.

～

"We should put some of these up on the walls." Meg flipped through another stack of old photos, pausing to examine the backs of those that featured images of young women, before setting them in a pile on the table in the Inn's kitchen. After her hospital stay a few days ago, she was still taking it easy, so Celia had asked Shawn to bring down the boxes from the attic that contained memorabilia from the Inn's first century. Now, Meg and Celia combed through the boxes for any mention of Davina Carlsen, the woman who'd written the journal Meg had found. "At the very least, we should make digital copies of everything to preserve them."

Celia nodded and reached for the cup of coffee she'd set on the table as far away from the photos as possible. "I think that's a good idea."

"Which one?" Meg grinned at her. "Preserving them or putting them on the walls?"

"Both." Celia laughed, and Meg could tell she enjoyed being part of the mission to figure out the Davina Carlsen mystery. Besides, she looked like she could use some downtime. Although Celia had been eager to open the Inn and act as its official hostess for overnight guests, it was probably physically taxing for her after being out of the business for so long.

"How is everything going with the guests?" Meg asked. "I'd be happy to help check them in."

"I think I can handle greeting them when they arrive and setting out pastries and coffee in the morning," Celia said dryly. "I may not be a spring chicken, but I'm not in the grave yet."

Meg's eyes widened. She hadn't meant to offend the elderly woman. "Oh, I just meant I didn't have that much to do, so if you needed anything..."

Celia's lips cracked into a smile. "I know you didn't mean anything, honey, and I appreciate your concern." She looked around the kitchen and out into the hallway. "Honestly, it feels good to be needed around here again.

There were so many years where it was just me and Pebbles bumbling around by ourselves." She smiled at her dog, who was lying on his pet bed next to the table. Upon hearing his name, Pebbles lifted his head, but laid back down when no treats were offered. "You know, I should be asking you how you're doing. You gave all of us quite a scare on Saturday night."

"I know. I'm sorry." Meg inhaled slowly through her nostrils, allowing the deep-breathing technique to calm her nerves.

She'd had to scrub herself down in the shower several times when she got home on Sunday before finally managing to get the stench of stale smoke out of her hair. She may not have been able to smell the acrid scent anymore, but thoughts of the fire and her guilt over not being able to stop it still intruded frequently into her thoughts. Taylor had left several messages for her, asking her if she was okay, but she hadn't called him back. The last she'd heard, he wasn't scheduled to fly back from California until that evening, so she figured she had a little time to figure out what she was going to say to him.

How was she going to face Taylor after she'd let Lara burn down the Lodge's kitchen? Having Meg take over the kitchen while he was on vacation had been a huge gesture of faith in her abilities, and she'd let him down. Maybe it was time to accept Theo's offer to sail the San Juan Islands with him. Getting away from Willa Bay for a few months might be exactly what she needed.

"You seem like you have a lot on your mind," Celia observed. "Do you want to talk about it?"

Meg shook her head. "No, not really. I just have some decisions to make."

Celia nodded sagely. "Well, let me know if you change your mind. I've been told I'm a good listener." She patted

Meg's hand, then returned to the stack of photos in front of her.

Meg thought she'd reached the last image in her current handful of photos, but it didn't feel right in her hand. The hair stood up on the back of her neck as she looked more closely, then eased her fingernail between two pieces of photo paper stuck together and carefully peeled them apart.

Hidden behind the first image was a sepia-toned portrait of a man, woman, and two children sitting on the steps of the Inn's gazebo. Meg flipped to the other side. In neat, but fading handwriting were the words, *Thomas and Birgitta Carlsen and their two children, Davina, age 12 and Lolly, age 6 months. August 1921.*

Meg sucked in her breath. "Celia. I think I found her."

Celia scooted her chair closer. "Thomas and Birgitta," she said, rolling the names over her tongue like she was tasting them. "I'm not familiar with them. Maybe they were guests at the Inn?"

"I don't know." Meg took a closer look at the family picture. The baby, Lolly, perched on the woman's lap, her chubby legs peeking out from the ruffled skirt of a white dress. Davina sat on the step below her parents, leaning against her father's legs as she smiled at the camera. She wore a long, pale dress and a strand of round beads hung around her neck. Her blonde hair had been bobbed, with precisely cut bangs across her forehead and a giant bow atop her head. "1921. This was taken about five years before the journal entries, so if they were guests, they must have come here annually."

Celia nodded. "That would make sense. Many families vacationed at the same resort in Willa Bay every year, often with standing reservations for a certain week or specific cottage."

They both peered at the photo and Meg couldn't stop herself from thinking about twelve-year-old Davina. Was she interested in cooking at that age, or was that something that had developed later? Meg was in the middle of imagining Davina and Lolly making sandcastles on the beach when her phone rang. Her whole body stiffened in response and her breath caught. Was it Taylor again?

She flipped over the phone and let out a long sigh. Not Taylor. She didn't recognize the phone number, but it had a Seattle area code. "Hello?"

"Hi," said a woman on the other end. "May I speak with Meg, please?"

"Speaking." Meg readied herself to hang up on a telemarketer.

"My name is Penny, and I'm calling to see if you would be interested in appearing on Coffee Talk Seattle. One of our producers covered the Inn's grand opening, and he couldn't stop raving about the food. When he spoke with the caterers, he was told they were recipes you'd found in the barn on the property." She paused to take a breath, then continued. "We would love to have you come on the show to teach us how to make one of the recipes. It would be such a great local-interest piece."

Pressure built in Meg's chest, squeezing her lungs to the point where she had to concentrate to breathe. She loved cooking, but her job was usually behind the scenes. This would entail teaching someone else to cook a recipe and would have the added stress of being filmed. Was she up to it?

Celia stared at her with concern and Meg smiled to let her know everything was okay. The tension eased from Celia's face, but it reminded Meg that all of them had a lot to lose if the Inn wasn't a success. An appearance on

Coffee Talk Seattle would be fantastic free publicity for their new business.

"I'd love to share the recipes on Coffee Talk. When did you want me to come in?" Meg had to work hard to steady the pitch of her words.

"Would next Monday, September fourteenth work?" Penny asked.

Next week? Meg's gut twisted at the thought of being on camera in front of the whole region. With a specific date, it was frighteningly real. "That would be great," she eked out.

"Great," Penny echoed. "We'll be in touch with you later this week with more details. I'm looking forward to meeting you on Monday."

"You too," Meg said automatically. They said their goodbyes and Penny hung up.

"So? Who was that?" Celia asked. "You look like you swallowed a goldfish."

"I feel like I swallowed a goldfish, or maybe a frog," Meg admitted. "It was someone from Coffee Talk Seattle. They want me to come in next Monday and show them how to prepare one of the recipes from the journal." Her gaze strayed to the Carlsen family photo in front of her. Seventeen-year-old Davina never could have imagined her recipes would one day be broadcast to thousands of people around the area.

"That's wonderful! I love that show." Celia searched Meg's face. "You do want to do it, right?"

Meg nodded. "I'm not a fan of the idea of being on television, but I'll get over it." The shock was wearing off and she was starting to see it could be a fun experience. The barn restaurant may be a far-off dream, but new opportunities were sprouting up for her all over. She stilled. The sailboat trip with Theo—he'd be long gone by next Monday.

"What is it, dear?" Celia cocked her head to the side.

Meg told her about Theo's offer and the conflict with being on the morning show.

"Oh." Celia sat back in her chair and sipped her coffee. "That is quite a pickle."

"Yep." Meg picked up the photo of Davina's family and focused on it. They looked so happy, sitting together in front of the gazebo. Life must have been so much easier in those days.

"Are you going to call them back and tell them you can't do the show?" Celia asked.

"I don't know." Meg set the portrait down and buried her head in her hands.

Celia put her arm around Meg and hugged her close. "What do you want to do?"

Meg laughed sharply. "I wish I knew."

"Do you want to go with Theo?" Celia asked. "It's a big commitment to go with him for a few months. I wouldn't want to do something like that without strong feelings for a man." She peered at Meg. "Do you love him?"

Love hadn't been something Meg had considered before. She and Theo had always kept things casual, but was she ready to take their relationship to the next level? And even if she was ready, was going away with him worth giving up the morning show appearance? He had demonstrated his commitment to her by visiting her in the hospital, but was that enough?

Meg stared blindly at the photos in front of her. "I don't know."

It wasn't just about Theo and the boat trip. Thinking about the night she'd spent in the hospital had brought up the memory of seeing the man in the hallway and wishing it was Taylor. He'd been so supportive of her dreams for the barn and now he'd lost the restaurant he loved—and it was all her fault. Now, while he was hurting, she was being offered a chance of a lifetime to share her passion for cooking on live television. How was any of this fair?

16

Tia

Tia parked in front of the fourplex apartment building she'd lived in for the last six months, got out of the car, and popped open the trunk to retrieve her groceries. She'd finally had a day off, and spent it running errands, including getting her hair cut for the first time since she'd moved here and long-overdue grocery shopping. The contents of her refrigerator were down to a few squishy tomatoes and a pack of sliced deli ham. With her busy work schedule, she'd been living on cheap fast food and leftovers that clients didn't want after events. It may not have been an ideal diet, but she was saving money.

She'd splurged a little at the grocery store and bought her favorite mint chocolate-chip ice cream to enjoy out on her small balcony as an after-dinner treat. They were entering the second week of September, and the summer weather was still going strong in the Pacific Northwest. Temperatures were forecasted to reach the high seventies that afternoon. Usually, she'd tidy up her apartment on her days off, but she'd been so busy lately that she hadn't had time to make much of a mess, so she intended to make good use of her free time by sitting on her balcony with a big bowl of ice cream and a good book.

A soft breeze ruffled Tia's hair as she opened the trunk of her sedan to retrieve her groceries, and she brushed it back with one hand, marveling as her fingers slid through the thick strands with ease. The hairstylist had chopped off several inches, leaving it to swing in a neat line just above her shoulders. The new style made her head feel lighter, and had somehow eased some of the built-up tension in her neck.

She rubbed her hand along the nape of her neck. Until she'd taken the opportunity to relax today, she hadn't realized how much stress she'd been under with the Inn's grand opening and all of the events they'd hosted in the last few weeks. Working as an event coordinator during the busy summer season wasn't easy, but she wouldn't have traded it for anything.

She plucked the grocery bags from the trunk and carried them to her front door, the canvas handles digging into her fingers. She carefully set them on the ground, unlocked her front door and stepped inside. Before she could turn back to grab the groceries, a realization stopped her in her tracks.

Dread gnawed at her insides as her brain tried to come up with a rational explanation for the water squishing up over the tops of her leather sandals. The carpet in her entry hall was as soggy as the towels she'd thrown in the tub after the plumbing fiasco at the Inn's grand opening. She took a deep breath and continued down the hall. Things didn't get any better as she went further inside.

Had she left the water running in the bathtub? She darted into the bathroom. A quick glance around revealed no open taps. Unfortunately, though, water was streaming from places it shouldn't have been. It rippled down the walls and dripped from the light fixture above, plopping onto Tia's head like fat raindrops from a thundercloud. The ceiling bulged ominously, and Tia backed away.

She ran into the living room, her feet making sucking sounds every time they came into contact with the floor. The ceiling in there was dry, but a few inches of water had accumulated on the floor, soaking the legs of her coffee table and the base of the couch. She flung open the bottom drawer of her desk, searching for the file with her landlord's information. Her meticulous record-keeping was coming in handy. She found what she was looking for and waded into the kitchen.

It wasn't any drier in there, so she sat on top of her two-person breakfast table, resting her feet on one of the oak chairs while she called the property management company.

"Hi, may I speak with Donald Denalian please?" Her gaze strayed to the water pooling on the scratched linoleum floor in front of the stove and she grimaced.

The receptionist transferred her to his office. "This is Donald, how may I help you?"

"Hi, this is Tia Ortiz. I live in the fourplex on Fifth Street."

"Oh yes," he replied pleasantly. "Of course. What can I do for you today?"

"I have a bit of a problem." She looked out at the living room, where the water level seemed to have risen at least a few inches in the last five minutes. It was way more than a bit of a problem. "My apartment is flooded. I think it's coming from upstairs."

"Flooded?" He asked in alarm. "How much water is there?"

"It's everywhere," she said flatly. "I think the ceiling in the bathroom is going to come down soon."

He sighed audibly. "Are you in the apartment now?"

"Yes."

"Get out of there and wait for me. I'll be to the building in less than ten minutes." The phone clicked off.

Tia climbed down from the table and accidentally knocked her purse onto the floor. She snatched it up before the water could seep through the faux leather to the contents inside and hurried toward the front hallway. Before she got there, she stopped in front of her bedroom door.

She almost didn't want to go in, afraid of what she'd might find. Slowly, she pushed on the half-closed door, displacing water in undulating currents as it swung open. It was about what she'd expected. When she'd leased the apartment, she hadn't been able to afford a bed frame, so she'd left the mattress on the floor. Now it was an island, her flowered comforter poking out from the center of a lake.

Flinging the wet purse strap over her head so it lay securely across her torso, she opened her plastic nightstand and removed a few personal items, then retrieved a photo album and some framed pictures from atop the dresser. When she'd moved to Willa Bay, she'd only brought with her what she could fit in her car. She may not have owned much of monetary value, but she would be heartbroken to lose a lifetime of memories. She loaded her arms with as much as she could carry and hurriedly brought it out to the car, repeating the process a few more times to remove her clothes, laptop and other important items. On her last trip, she paused at the front door to take one last look at her apartment.

Whatever was causing the flood hadn't stopped yet,

judging by the sound of running water coming from the bathroom. The apartment was almost a total loss at this stage. There was no way she was going to be able to save any of the furniture, and she didn't have renter's insurance. With so few belongings, it hadn't made sense to spend her already tight funds on insurance. But even used furniture had a price tag. It may have been from Goodwill and not in the best of shape, but it had been her furniture —her home. How was she going to replace everything?

She put the items she'd removed from her apartment into her car and set the groceries in the front passenger seat. As promised, her landlord arrived within ten minutes of her call. She greeted him and he entered her apartment. He emerged a minute later and ran around to the side of the building.

When he returned to where she was standing, his face was grim. "A pipe must have burst in the apartment upstairs. I've shut off the building's water."

He pulled out his phone and called his office, barking orders to his staff to notify the other tenants in the building and to call an emergency plumber. When he'd finished, he walked about ten feet away from her and dialed another number. From what he was saying, Tia figured it was the insurance company, and judging by his expression, the news wasn't good.

He shoved the phone into his pants pocket and turned back to her. "They're not going to be able to get anyone out here to assess the damage until tomorrow." He balled up his fists and closed his eyes briefly. "I'm sorry Ms. Ortiz." I've had things like this happen before and it's usually at least a month or two until the apartment is ready to inhabit again. He eyed her closed apartment door. "Is there anything you need to get out of there?"

She shook her head and gestured to the car. "No. I

only had a few things and I've got them in the car already." She looked toward her apartment. He'd confirmed her worst fears about the flood. Where was she going to live?

"Do you have family you can stay with for a few months?" he asked kindly.

"No." She bit her lip. "My family all lives in Texas."

He lightly snapped his fingers by his sides and his face contorted in deep thought. He sighed. "I wish I could help, but all of our rental units are full. It's the same story all over town. This couldn't have come at a worse time."

You're telling me, she thought. It wasn't his fault though. She pasted a smile on her face. "You know, I'm sure I'll be able to find something. Maybe one of my friends can put me up for a while." Whether she could impose on any acquaintances in this town, she didn't know, but she hoped to ease his distress.

He brightened. "Oh, good. I'm glad you have someone in the area. And I'll make sure to let you know as soon as I find out a timeline from the insurance company."

A white van with the words "Paulsen Plumbing" emblazoned across the side pulled up to the curb, and a middle-aged man with a slight paunch exited the vehicle. "Hi. Did one of you call for a plumber?"

Donald nodded and motioned for the man to follow him. "Come with me."

Both men entered her apartment, and Tia took that as her cue to leave. She got into her car and turned on the air conditioning, then slumped in her seat. She'd been calm and in charge of the situation while she was busy calling the landlord and getting her belongings out of the apartment. Now that there was nothing left for her to do, her sense of control slipped. Next to her, condensation beaded on top of the half gallon of ice cream. If she didn't get that into a freezer soon, it would also be ruined.

What she really wanted was reassurance that things would be okay, so she called her mom. She wasn't convinced it was the best choice, but she needed to hear a familiar voice.

"Mom?" Tia asked, turning on the speakerphone and placing it on the dashboard when Marta Ortiz answered.

"Honey?" her mother asked. "Are you alright?"

"Kind of." She sniffled as her face crumpled and the tears began to flow.

"Something's wrong. What happened? Did you get robbed? I always said you shouldn't be alone out there." Her mother's voice rose with concern, even as she admonished Tia.

"No, Mom. I didn't get robbed."

Calling her mom had been a bad idea. The apartment flood was just one more nail in the coffin of her independence. The car's air conditioner kicked in full blast and she shivered. Turning the fan down, she leaned closer to the window to feel the sun's warmth. Her head throbbed, either from the sudden change in temperature or from her reluctance to admit to her mother that she was now homeless. She sat upright and the pulsing in her head ceased.

"Well, what is it?" Her mother asked impatiently. "You never call me unless something's wrong."

Tia clenched her jaw and breathed in the icy cool air flowing out of the vent in front of her. "A pipe burst in the apartment above mine and flooded my apartment. I've lost almost everything."

"Okay, that's it," her mother said, as if everything was settled. "It's time you admit that you can't make it on your own. You need to come back home. If you'd like, I'm sure

Dad would be happy to fly out there and drive back with you."

"That won't be necessary. I'll be staying in Willa Bay." Tia didn't have a clue where she'd live, but she'd figure it out. She for sure wouldn't be moving back to Texas.

"That's ridiculous." Her mother's voice rang with indignation. "You don't have a support system out there. You should be here with the rest of the family."

"I have friends," Tia said stubbornly. "I can make it on my own."

"We'll see about that," her mother said.

"Yep." Tia gripped the steering wheel tightly. "We will."

"Tia, you know we love you, right?" Marta said. "We just want what's best for you."

"I know." Even with the air conditioning running, the car was starting to smell like melted mint ice cream. "Mom, I've got to go. I'll call you and let you know when I find a new place to stay."

"Thank you," Marta said stiffly before hanging up.

Tia knew very few people in Willa Bay, so she called Zoe, who always seemed to have the answers.

"Hey, how's it going?" Zoe asked. "Are you having fun on your day off?"

"Not exactly." Tia told her about the damage to her apartment.

"Oh no!" Zoe said. "That's way worse than what happened at the Inn's grand opening."

"Yeah." Tia looked at the backseat through the rearview mirror. All of her worldly possessions were in her car, just like when she'd moved to Willa Bay. "The landlord says I can't move back in for at least a month, if then."

"Do you have a place to stay?" Zoe asked.

"No." Tia felt like she was about to cry again. "I was hoping you might have an idea."

"I do," Zoe said brightly. "You can come and stay with me, at least until we can figure something better out. My cottage isn't big, but you can have the couch."

Tia's heart lifted. "Really? You'd let me stay with you?" It wasn't a permanent solution, but it was miles above where she'd been a minute ago.

"Of course," Zoe said. "What are friends for?"

Friends. At the moment, that was the nicest thing Tia had ever heard. She looked over at the groceries.

"Do you by chance have room in the freezer for a half-gallon of ice cream?"

Zoe laughed. "There's always room for ice cream."

"Thanks, Zoe. I'll be there in ten minutes."

"See you then."

They hung up, and Tia started driving, happy to know that she *did* have friends and a support system in Willa Bay.

17

Meg

"And then, after freezing it overnight, you end up with this." Meg opened the canary-yellow freezer door in Coffee Talk Seattle's demonstration kitchen and pulled out the icebox cake she'd made. She tilted the clear glass baking pan to the side to allow the live studio audience a glimpse of the rippled chocolate and whipped cream confection. Her efforts were met with *oohs* and *ahs* from the crowd. "Looks delicious, doesn't it?"

The audience murmured in agreement.

"Well folks," Demi Andle, one of the show hosts said. "We've got a treat in store for you today. Our lovely guest chef was kind enough to make enough icebox cake for everyone!" Demi flashed a big TV smile, teeth gleaming brightly behind hot pink lipstick that matched her ruffled blouse.

The murmur turned into wild cheering, and Meg grinned widely. As they began serving dessert to the entire audience, row by row, she stepped off of the set, stopping in the green room backstage where she could see everyone's reactions as they tasted the treat. Judging by their faces, her cake—or, rather, Davina's cake—was a huge success.

Being in front of an audience had been both terrifying and exhilarating at the same time. She'd had a touch of stage fright when she'd first arrived, but Demi and her co-host, Charles, had made her feel as comfortable as though she were cooking at home for her family. Thank goodness she'd accepted the opportunity to appear on the show. It would be wonderful publicity for the Inn and her future restaurant.

However, it was an opportunity that had come at a cost. Meg had undergone hours of soul-searching as she struggled to choose between going with Theo to sail the San Juan Islands and staying in Willa Bay to be on the TV show and continue readying the barn for extensive renovations. In the end, she'd taken Celia's advice to heart.

While she'd enjoyed spending time with Theo, she'd finally admitted to herself that he wasn't someone she could see herself settling down with. After reaching that conclusion, she'd had a long conversation with him, and they'd come to the mutual decision to end their relationship. Looking back, it had been a surprisingly clean break, which further solidified her belief that he wasn't the right man for her. Even with that certainty, she still missed his companionship.

"Meg!" Demi called out to her as she entered the green room. "You did a great job. The audience loved your cake and loved you even more."

Meg felt a telltale blush work its way upward from her neck. She looked down at her feet, which were clad in white leather sandals she'd bought for the occasion, then forced herself to meet the show host's eyes. "Thank you. I had fun today."

Demi tapped her finger against her lips. "What would you say to being on the show again? Maybe once or twice a month?"

Meg gaped, the woman's suggestion stealing her breath away for a moment. It had been one thing to appear on live TV once, but to do it on an ongoing basis? That was another case entirely.

Demi laughed. "I know, being on TV takes some getting used to." She studied Meg carefully. "But I think you have a knack for it. Your sense of timing is impeccable."

"Really?" Meg stared at her, trying hard to keep her mouth shut.

Demi nodded. "Yes. Plus, they were eating up the story about the recipes coming from an old journal you found in a barn. That, in itself, is a good human-interest piece."

Meg would never have guessed the day she and Taylor found Davina's journal that it would have such an impact on her life. The lucky discovery had not only given her a connection to the Inn's past, but a spot on local TV, and some interesting recipes she planned to serve in her future restaurant.

She smiled. "I'd love to come back on the show."

"Wonderful," Demi gushed. "I'll have our producers contact you." She whirled and exited the green room in a flash of pink.

Still mildly shocked, Meg went to retrieve her purse from the cubbies along the wall of the green room. When she turned back around, she did a double take. A tall man stood in the entrance. This time, she wasn't imagining his presence.

"Taylor!" She put her hand to her heart. "You scared me."

"Sorry." He gave her a guilty look. "I didn't mean to. I just wanted to catch you before you left so I could congratulate you on how well you did."

Her face heated up again. "You saw the show?" She'd been so determined to not let the presence of an audience scare her that she'd immersed herself in her cooking. The Queen of England could have been there and she wouldn't have noticed.

"I did." He smiled. "And you were fantastic."

"Thanks." She gripped her purse tightly. It had been over a week since the fire, and this was the first time she'd talked to him. She'd put off the difficult task for as long as possible, but now it was to time to face her fears. "Um, about the fire..." She looked up at him and searched his face, hoping he didn't blame her for what had happened.

He cocked his head to the side. "What about it?"

Not wanting to have this conversation inside the studio, she had him follow her out to the parking lot, where she drank in huge gulps of fresh air to quell her nerves.

"Meg. What is it?" He put his hands on her shoulders and turned her to face him straight on.

"I'm so sorry about what happened," she whispered.

"Sorry?" He raised his eyebrows. "What for?"

She studied her sandals again. "I tried to put out the fire, but I couldn't stop it from spreading."

"Meg. It wasn't your fault." He peered at her. "If we're going to place any blame, it should be on Lara."

"But you trusted me with your kitchen. I should have made sure she was being safe, but I assumed she knew what she was doing." She frowned. "I assumed wrong."

"It wasn't your fault," he repeated. His hands dropped

from her shoulders, grazing her bare skin as he pulled her close. She shivered at his touch but relaxed against him, dissolving into sobs as she relived the fire and guilt all over again. "No one blames you."

She stepped back and met his gaze. "I blame me. The kitchen was my responsibility."

He sighed. "Please. Stop worrying about it. Once George gets the insurance situation resolved, we'll have the Lodge's restaurant up and running in no time." He gave her an impish smile. "I never liked that range anyway. It was never any good at regulating its temperature."

"Really?" She hoped he was telling her the truth.

"Really." He patted her arm reassuringly, then looked around the parking lot. "Is Theo here? Zoe told me about the cooking show. I know she and Cassie really wanted to come, but they both had to work. I figured Theo would be here though."

"Nope. He's somewhere in the San Juan Islands." She briefly closed her eyes as an image popped into her head of Theo's sailboat cutting through the channels between the lushly forested islands.

She sighed and opened her eyes, her heart filling with warmth at the sight of Taylor. Only a true friend would both forgive her for burning down his restaurant and show up to see her appear on TV in the middle of the morning. The sailing trip would have been nice, but she had a lot going for her back in Willa Bay too.

"Ah. I bet he's sad to have missed you on the morning show. How long is he gone for?" Taylor inquired politely.

She shrugged. "I have no clue. We broke up before he left."

"Oh." An odd expression crossed Taylor's face, but she couldn't make out what he was thinking. "I'm sorry to hear that."

"Me too, but it was for the best. He wanted to continue seeing the world, and my life is here in Willa Bay." It really had been for the best. Zoe had mentioned to her again that if she finished clearing out the barn soon, they could start on the renovations instead of moving on to the cottages, which had been the original plan. Now that she could see a light at the end of the tunnel, Meg didn't plan to let anything jeopardize the barn's renovation timeline. If everything went according to schedule, they may even be able to open the restaurant just after Christmas.

She shaded her face from the sun's rays and looked up at Taylor. "Well, I'd better get going. I told Zoe I'd meet her and Cassie at Wedding Belles for lunch."

He nodded and stuck his thumbs through the belt loops on his dark jeans. "I hope you have fun. And Meg?"

"Yeah?"

"You really did a great job on the show. I was proud of you."

Happiness flooded every part of her body. She'd always admired Taylor's skills in the kitchen, and to receive praise from him was everything. "Thank you." A thought occurred to her. "Hey, since you don't need to hurry off to the Lodge, would you like to join the girls and me for lunch?"

He hesitated. "Are you sure that would be okay with them?"

She laughed, feeling lighter than she had in days. "They won't mind a bit."

They got into their own cars and drove separately to the riverside cafe on Willa Bay's Main Street. He waited for her by the door, and they entered Wedding Belles together. Cassie waved eagerly at them from the window table that she and Zoe had secured. Meg hadn't been able to wait until she saw them in person, and had called both of them on her way home to fill them in on her experience being on TV. She'd also given them a heads up that Taylor would be joining them for lunch.

Meg walked proudly over to her friends and sat down, feeling as confident as a movie star.

"Hey, Taylor," Zoe said. "I'm glad you could join us."

"Me too," he said as he took a seat next to Cassie, across from Meg. "It's been a while since we had the whole Lodge gang together. I miss seeing the three of you." He frowned. "Lara and the new staff just aren't the same."

Cassie wrinkled her nose. "I don't see how you can work there with her, especially after she burned down your restaurant."

Meg watched Taylor carefully as she sipped the ice water the waitress had just dropped off at their table. It really hit the spot after the car ride back from the television studio in Seattle.

He took a long drink of water as well, then set the glass down on the table and said slowly, "I don't really have a choice about working with Lara. She's George's daughter, so she's there to stay. But I do think I need to have an honest conversation with both of them about my expectations."

"Uh, yeah." Zoe laughed. "They'll walk all over you if you don't watch out."

He hung his head. "I know." He slugged down more water and looked out the window at the deck and the river below.

The conversation had taken a downturn and Meg noticed that Taylor's jovial demeanor had vanished, so she changed the topic. "So, what else is new? Did I miss anything exciting at the Inn today?" She'd left for Seattle early in the morning and hadn't had time to stop in at the

Inn first, although she planned to work on cleaning the barn that afternoon.

"Actually, yes. Kind of," Zoe said. The waitress came by to take their orders, then Zoe continued. "Tia's apartment flooded."

"Seriously?" Cassie's eyes widened. "Was it bad?"

Zoe nodded. "She lost almost everything she owned. Apparently, a pipe in the bathroom ceiling burst."

"Oh no." Meg's life was looking better and better by the second. "Where's she going to stay?" The real estate market in Willa Bay was both expensive and tight, two reasons why Meg lived above her parents' garage.

"I said she could live with me," Zoe said. "It'll be a little cramped, but she doesn't know many people in town and didn't have anywhere else to go."

"That's awful." Meg was quiet, thinking about how it would feel to lose everything in her apartment.

"Could she move into one of the cottages?" Cassie asked. "Weren't you going to work on them next?"

Zoe shook her head. "No, we decided to fix up the barn first. It was only fair to Meg since she's helped so much with the rest of the property."

Taylor looked at Meg and smiled. "Once the restoration is complete, it's going to be perfect for a restaurant. Willa Bay won't know what hit it."

She shot him a look of gratitude. Unlike Theo, Taylor understood her vision for the barn and what it meant to her. Looking back, that should have been a clue that Theo wasn't right for her. If he couldn't be supportive of her dream, he couldn't be supportive of her.

"You can't divert some of the construction team to one of the cottages?" Cassie asked. "I mean, I don't really know how it all works, but it can't take up that many resources, right?"

Zoe frowned. "It's more a matter of logistics. If we start on the cottages, we need to finish that project before moving on to the barn. I feel bad about it, but having Tia live in one of the cottages just isn't going to work. I'll help her figure out a long-term solution."

But the work on the barn hadn't started yet. Meg's chest constricted as her thoughts collided against each other. Tia had been so kind to her at the Inn's grand opening, comforting Meg as she panicked about how Davina's recipes would be received. Now, the other woman had lost everything and was essentially homeless.

Meg inhaled deeply and slowly let out her breath. She felt Taylor's eyes on her face even before she looked over at him. His gaze was heavy with compassion, seeming to know what she was going to do not long after she'd come to the realization herself.

Her words came out in a rush before she could change her mind. "I think we should postpone the barn renovation and work on the cottages first. Tia needs a place to live, and it just makes sense for her to live on the property since she's there all the time anyway."

"Are you serious?" Zoe's eyes drilled into her. "You want to do the cottages first? Once we start on the project, we can't change our minds."

"I know." Her stomach twisted at the thought of pushing the dream of having her own restaurant even further into the future.

Taylor reached across the table and squeezed Meg's hand. "Are you sure this is what you want?" he asked softly.

She nodded. "I'm sure."

Everything was happening so fast. Uncertainty built up in her chest and she fought to tamp it down. Like he understood the conflict running through her, Taylor didn't let go of her. She stared at her hand in his and wondered if he could feel her trembling.

Cassie averted her eyes, but not before Meg caught the smirk on her face. Her friend had long proclaimed that Taylor had feelings for Meg. Meg had never believed her, but with the way he was looking at her now... He gave her a small smile of reassurance that made Meg's heart pound. Had Cassie been right all along?

Zoe removed her phone from her purse and stood from the table. "I'll let Shawn know we've had a change of plans."

As she passed by, Taylor took his hand off of Meg's. Immediately, she experienced a sense of loss that was greater than she'd felt on the last day she'd seen Theo. She casually pulled her hand back and busied herself with digging through her bag for an unknown object.

In the space of a few minutes, her life had spun around like a globe on its axis. She should have been deflated by the postponement of the barn remodel, but her nerves buzzed with the feelings Taylor's touch had evoked, clouding her judgment.

As much as she wanted to help Tia, had she made the right decision? Should she run after Zoe and tell her not to call Shawn? Meg turned to look for Zoe. Her friend had just reached the door, her progress through the restaurant slowed by the lunch crowds. If Meg hurried, she could still catch Zoe before it was too late to change her mind.

18

Taylor

After they'd finished their lunch at Wedding Belles, Taylor said goodbye to Meg, Zoe, and Cassie and drove to the Willa Bay Lodge. So far, the day had been an emotional roller coaster. He'd gone to the taping of Coffee Talk Seattle to wish Meg well and let her know he planned to move back to San Diego, but now he wasn't so sure of that plan.

From the moment he'd heard about the kitchen fire and Meg's injuries, he'd known he was in love with her. As much as he'd tried to suppress those feelings, they weren't going away. He'd caught the next flight back to Seattle the night of the fire, but it had been early morning when he'd arrived in Willa Bay, and well past visiting hours at the hospital.

When he'd woken up on Sunday morning, his first thought had been to head to the hospital to see Meg. However, a night's rest had brought the realization that he couldn't see her in person—it would be too painful to see

Theo there at her bedside. Since then, he'd tried to call Meg several times, but his voicemails had met an empty silence.

George had notified Taylor and the rest of the restaurant staff that they weren't allowed in the building until the insurance adjustors had assessed the damage. Taylor had gotten the impression that George didn't hold out much hope for the restaurant coming back online for at least a month or two. Since Taylor had come to the conclusion that he needed to resign from his position at the Lodge, it had seemed like perfect timing. Starting anew in San Diego wouldn't be easy and he'd probably have to take a lower-ranking job, but he had contacts that could help him find something. Although he loved his current job as head chef at the Lodge, he needed a personal life too, and that wasn't going to happen in Willa Bay.

It had been too much for him to be around Meg while she was dating Theo. But, now that he knew they'd broken up, Taylor wasn't sure where that left him and the deep feelings he had for her. She was no longer romantically involved with someone else, but would she ever reciprocate Taylor's affections?

At the Lodge, he strode down the long hallway and rapped on the open door to George's office, still unsure about his decision to leave Willa Bay.

George looked up at him and motioned for him to come in. "Taylor. It's good to see you. I wanted to have a chat with you about the kitchen repairs." He peered at something on his computer monitor.

Taylor's mind buzzed. If he was going to tell George he was quitting, it was now or never. "I've been wanting to talk to you too."

George eyed him quizzically. "About the repairs?"

Taylor shook his head. "No." He paused, searching for the right words. "I need to talk to you about my job."

George leaned back in his chair, giving Taylor his full attention now. "Oh?"

Taylor took a deep breath. "I need to talk to you about my role in the kitchen, and how difficult it is for me to successfully manage the restaurant with Lara as our pastry chef."

George raised his eyebrows but said nothing.

Taylor may come out of this meeting unemployed, but at least he would know he'd tried to make things better for the future. If he was going to stay at the Lodge, something had to be done about Lara. "Respectfully, sir, I know she's your daughter, but she makes life miserable for all of us in the kitchen."

George held up his hand and cut in, "She didn't mean to start the fire."

"I'm not talking about the fire," Taylor said. "Although that's just a symptom of the problem. She constantly makes messes and assumes that other people will clean them up. One day last month, she neglected to make the desserts I needed for the evening's dinner service. She told me she was too busy making cakes for her decorating business to do her job at the Lodge." The memory of his phone call with her that night made him seethe inside.

"That doesn't sound like Lara." George leaned on the desk and tented his hands.

Taylor cringed inwardly, but plowed ahead. "Those weren't the only incidents. Maybe it's not something you usually see with her, but that's how she's been ever since she started in my kitchen. I can't keep working here if things don't change."

He stared at George defiantly. If the older man wanted to fire him, so be it. At least he'd finally been honest about the situation in the kitchen. He'd already lost Cassie and Meg, in part to Lara's behavior. If he was going to stay in Willa Bay, he couldn't afford to lose any more good kitchen staff.

"I see." George turned and thoughtfully regarded the photo of his family that perched on a shelf behind him, then turned back to Taylor with sadness in his eyes. "You know, Taylor, I've always respected you and your work. I'll have a talk with Lara." He sighed deeply. "She needs to respect your authority in the kitchen. Being my daughter doesn't give her the right to not complete her job requirements."

Taylor braced himself by gripping the top of the chair in front of him, attempting to stop the shaking in his legs. Although no one would describe him as meek, he'd never expected to confront his boss about Lara. Complaining to someone about their daughter usually wasn't a great career move.

"Thank you," Taylor said simply. "I'd appreciate that."

George nodded, then gazed at his computer and frowned. "I have a phone call I need to make, but I'll follow up with Lara about this. You and I can chat later this week about the kitchen renovations."

"Thank you," Taylor said again.

George picked up the phone receiver and Taylor hurried out of the office, closing the door behind him. He peeked into the kitchen, and sucked in his breath. Yellow caution tape stretched across half of the kitchen, blocking Taylor from his own office. The acrid odor of smoke hung in the air and one entire wall was completely charred. The kitchen had been beautiful once, but now it lay in ruins. He ducked out of the building and strode toward the parking lot.

Leaning against his car, he gulped in a lungful of fresh

air, then reached into his pocket for his phone. He needed to talk to someone about everything, preferably someone with strong opinions about his life—like his sister.

It rang twice before Susanna answered. "Taylor! I was hoping it was you. How is your restaurant? Is Meg okay?"

"Meg's fine. She inhaled some smoke, but they released her from the hospital by the next morning. The kitchen, not so much." His stomach clenched, thinking about the condition of his restaurant. He loved that kitchen—had loved making it his own. Now it looked like it had lost a fight with a blow torch. "However, I did have a long conversation with my boss. I told him he needed to choose between me or his daughter, who was the pastry chef who started the fire." He laughed. "Catching my kitchen on fire isn't my only complaint about her, but I can't help resenting her for that too."

Suzanne gasped in surprise. "What did your boss say when you gave him the ultimatum?"

"He chose me, I think." Taylor's voice shook with wonder. How had that even happened? He opened the car door and collapsed onto the sun-warmed fabric covering the driver's seat. "He's going to have a talk with his daughter about how she's been acting."

"So, you're saying you're going to stay in Willa Bay?" Her voice rang with concern. "Are you sure that's the best thing for you to do with the whole Meg situation? It sounded like you really care for her."

Taylor pictured Meg's face, and he suddenly felt lighter, as though the stress of the day had melted away. "Actually, Meg and her boyfriend broke up."

"What? Well are you going to go for her?" Susanna sounded so elated that Taylor could almost see the huge smile on her face.

"I don't know." Was this the right time to tell Meg how

he felt, after she'd just broken up with her boyfriend? His heart hammered so rapidly that he feared it would leap right out of his rib cage. If he waited for the "right" time, she could very well meet someone else before he got up the nerve to tell her how much he cared for her. "Yes," he said softly. "I'm going to tell her."

He leaned back in the seat. That was it. Now that he'd verbally committed to confessing his feelings to Meg, his sister was not going to let it go until he went through with it.

"How are you going to tell her?"

He chuckled. Susanna must be on the edge of her seat by now. He paused to consider his sister's question. More than anything, he wanted to do something nice for Meg. She'd put aside all of her past grievances and unpleasant memories of working at the Lodge to cover for him so he could attend Diana's wedding. Now, he had an opportunity to return the favor.

Maybe, just maybe, it would help him show her the depth of his love for her. If his grand gesture brought them closer together, it would be wonderful. But, if she didn't reciprocate his feelings, at least she'd know how much he cared for her and valued her friendship.

19

Tia

When Tia arrived at the Inn on Saturday morning, Meg and Celia were already drinking coffee at the kitchen table.

"Good morning!" Tia said as she walked over to the cupboard and grabbed a pink ceramic mug emblazoned with a rainbow ending in a pot of gold. With the way things were going in her life, she could use a little luck.

Celia twisted in her chair to face Tia. "Morning, dear."

"How are things at Zoe's house?" Meg sipped her coffee as she waited for Tia's response.

Tia shrugged. "Okay, I guess. Her couch is pretty comfortable, but I feel like I'm getting in her way." She poured coffee into her cup, then set it on the counter to cover her mouth as she yawned. Zoe's couch may be comfortable, but sleeping in the living room with the refrigerator in the adjoining kitchen humming all night didn't make for restful sleep. She brought her coffee over to the table and sat in a chair facing Celia. "I appreciate her letting me crash there for a while though." The corners of her mouth tugged downward at the thought of needing to find a permanent place to live. Cheap apartments in Willa Bay weren't terribly plentiful.

"Well, I'm glad you're settling in." Celia beamed at her. "If there's anything you need from me, remember I'm just up the road from you."

"Thanks." Tia flashed Celia a smile. In the short time she'd worked at the Inn, she'd come to appreciate the elderly woman's kindness and compassion. "How is everything going this morning with the overnight guests?" Several of the rooms had been rented to guests of the small wedding they'd be hosting that afternoon.

"They've been fed and watered." Celia chuckled, deepening the laugh lines in her wrinkled cheeks. "Seriously, though, they've had their continental breakfast, and everyone seems pleased with the accommodations."

"Good." Tia's coffee had cooled enough to drink, and she took a long swig of it, eager for the caffeine infusion.

Meg got up to refill her coffee, then returned to the table. "Celia was just telling me that she found a birth certificate for the woman who used to own this house, Lorraine Olsen."

"Oh?" Tia wasn't sure of the significance of this information.

"Apparently Lorraine was a Carlsen before she married," Meg said.

"We found a photo of the woman who wrote the journal, Davina Carlsen, with her parents and younger sister, Lolly," Celia said. "Lolly used to be a common nickname for Lorraine, so we think there's a good chance Lorraine Olsen was Davina's younger sister."

"Really?" Tia asked. "I thought she didn't have any

family." She turned to Celia. "Isn't that how you ended up with the Inn?"

Celia bobbed her head. "It is. I never knew she had any kin either." She shrugged, her bony shoulders forming sharp angles under her white knit cardigan.

"For all we know, Davina died years before Lorraine ever took over management of the Inn from her parents." Meg's eyes clouded over, as though mourning the long-ago death of the journal's author.

Celia patted Meg's hand. "I hope we'll be able to find out more about her."

"Me too." Meg rubbed her thumb along her mug's handle. "I can't help wondering about who she was and what happened to her. It almost feels like we're connected through her recipes."

"I'm sure she'd appreciate the sentiment." Celia pushed her chair back and wrapped her fingers around the metal arms of her walker, lifting herself to a standing position. "Now, I'd better get to the front desk in case anyone has questions for me." She paused, and focused dewy eyes on them. "You know, it feels good to be useful again."

Tia and Meg exchanged smiles.

"We couldn't do it without you," Meg said.

"Definitely not." Tia finished off her coffee and carried her mug and Celia's over to the sink. "We'd be sunk." She meant it too. Over the summer, a sudden closure of a local wedding venue had left clients struggling to find a replacement location on short notice. Without Celia's vast knowledge of the property and the community, there was no way they could have opened the Inn ahead of schedule.

"Well, I don't know about all that." Patches of pale pink appeared on Celia's cheeks. "But thank you for saying so." She directed her gaze at Tia. "I almost forgot. Shawn asked me to have you meet with him when you got in."

"Shawn did?" Tia couldn't keep the surprise from her voice. As Zoe's second-in-command for event planning, her duties didn't intersect too much with Shawn's role as the manager of renovations. Her blood ran cold. Had she done something wrong?

"Yes." Celia smiled peacefully at her. "He asked for you to meet him at Cottage Twenty."

"Okay..." This was getting more and more confusing. Why would he want to meet her at one of the abandoned cottages? It was about as far away from the event areas as she could get.

Meg seemed to sense her confusion and jumped to her feet. "I'll come with you. I wouldn't mind a walk before I get started on all the tasks Zoe's assigned to me for the day."

"Thanks." Tia shot her a grateful smile.

"I'll see you girls later," Celia called over her shoulder as she pushed her walker across the kitchen floor in the direction of the sink.

Tia and Meg left the kitchen and walked out the front door of the Inn. Earlier that morning there'd been a hint of the chilly autumn to come, but since then the sun had warmed the air to a pleasant temperature. Tia was quickly learning why the locals considered September to be one of the nicest months in the Pacific Northwest.

On the way to the cottage, the two of them chatted about the journal Meg had found and the recent flood at Tia's apartment. As they drew close enough to see the twentieth cottage at the end of the lane, Tia stopped. Meg paused as well, giving her a look that Tia couldn't quite interpret.

Tia stared at the cottage steps. Both Shawn and Zoe sat on the second step, with Shawn's toolbox nestled between his feet. A brand-new board had been nailed into place on the bottom step, the pale wood a sharp contrast to the weathered materials on the rest of the cottage. Ordinarily, Tia wouldn't have been surprised to see Shawn working on a project around the resort, but she knew they didn't plan to renovate the cottages until next spring. Why would he have taken the time to replace this step?

She turned to Meg. Her co-worker's lips quivered, like she was fighting to keep from smiling. Tia narrowed her eyes. "Am I missing something?"

Meg couldn't maintain the poker face anymore, and she chuckled a little. "Nope. Not missing anything." She gestured to Zoe and Shawn. "Maybe you should ask them."

"Are you just going to stand there?" Zoe called out. "Get over here!" Both she and Shawn wore huge grins.

Tia approached them, still fixated on the new step. She pointed at it. "Why are we meeting here? Did you need something from me?"

"Not at all," Shawn drawled.

"I don't understand." Tia couldn't do anything but stare at them.

Meg finally took pity on her. She came up beside Tia and put her arm around her shoulders. "How would you feel about moving into this cottage?"

"Uh." Tia eyed the peeling pink paint with a sinking sensation in the pit of her stomach. Did Zoe want her off her couch that badly? "I'm not sure."

The building wasn't in great shape, but she hadn't seen the inside. Maybe it wasn't as bad as the exterior. Still, it would take a lot of work to make it inhabitable.

She looked it over again and felt her excitement start to build.

What would it be like to live here? She'd always loved this cottage, with its peekaboo view of the water through the trees and private location at the end of the lane.

Shawn stood from the porch step and held out his hand to help Zoe up. They walked closer to Tia, stopping about two feet away.

"We really appreciate how much help you've been at the Inn." Zoe's gaze shot over to Meg, who nodded. "If you're interested, we'd like to start renovating the cottages next, starting with this one. As soon as it's done, you could move in."

"Really?" Tia asked. They barely knew her. Why would they do that for her? A little voice in her head told her just to be happy and not question it.

Zoe laughed. "Yeah. Really," she said. "Besides, if you live here, you'll be able to work more." She winked at Tia to show she was kidding.

Tia let herself give in to the dizzying happiness spreading throughout her body. But then a thought popped into her head that drenched her elation as if someone had thrown a bucket of cold water over her.

"What about the barn renovations?" She turned to face Meg. "I thought those were next on the list."

Meg gave her a small smile. "We've decided to postpone the barn renovations until we're done with the cottages."

Tia froze in place, staring at Meg. "Is this because of me? Because I needed a place to live?" She almost didn't want to ask, but she had to know the truth. After the words were out though, she realized how selfish they sounded. Of course they hadn't changed their plans just for her.

Meg hesitated and Tia's fears were confirmed. They *had* changed their plans to accommodate her. She didn't know whether to feel flattered or devastated to have squashed Meg's plans. The barn restaurant was incredibly important to Meg. Had she been included in the decision to alter the construction timeline?

"No, it wasn't completely because of you." Meg looked in the direction of the Inn and barn. "There's so much left to do in the barn before we start renovations. At this rate, I doubt I'll even be finished clearing it out before the cottages are refurbished."

Tia scrutinized Meg's face. "Are you sure you want to do this?"

Meg grinned. "I'm sure. With my new role on Coffee Talk Seattle, and everything going on with the Inn, this just isn't the right time to start on the barn. I'm going to use the extra time to make sure I know exactly what I want for the space."

With tears pooling in the corners of her eyes, Tia impulsively threw her arms around Meg. "Thank you."

Meg patted her back. "No problem." She stepped aside and grimaced at the cottage. "But I think we've got our work cut out for us to make this livable."

Shawn waved his hand in the air. "Eh, it looks worse than it really is." He pointed to the door. "Does anyone want to take a tour?"

A thrill shot through Tia and she nodded her head vigorously. "I know I do."

"Well, let's do it." Shawn climbed the porch steps and unlocked the door, letting it swing open. "The power's off out here, but that's an easy fix."

Tia and the others followed him inside. After her eyes adjusted to the dim light in the small entry, she tentatively made her way into the living room. The air was musty, but didn't contain the telltale reek of mold and mildew. Natural light shone through the big front window, illuminating the generously sized room and fireplace.

Meg, Zoe, and Shawn trailed behind Tia, letting her take it all in first. She quickened her pace, striding through to the kitchen in the back. With every step she took, she became more excited about the prospect of living there. The kitchen was dated, but, like the living room, in decent shape for not being used in over a decade.

She stopped in front of a dirty window to peer into the backyard. The grass was long, and the shrubs and weeds had long ago overtaken it, but she could see how it once had been, and what it could be in the future. They circled through the kitchen back into the hallway, and she peeked into the bathroom. A clawfoot tub sat under the casement window. She'd always wanted one of those.

Shawn cleared his throat. "The bedrooms are upstairs." He moved down the hallway, past the bathroom.

Tia hurried to catch up to him, and they all went upstairs. Shawn and Zoe seemed familiar with the layout, but from the way Meg was examining everything, she'd never been inside the cottage either. They reached the top of the stairs, exiting onto a landing bracketed by a door on each side.

"Wait, are there two bedrooms?" Tia asked. "I thought the cottages all had only one bedroom."

Shawn shook his head. "No. The ones closer to the Inn, like where Zoe and I live, are smaller. Down at this end, most were built for families and have at least two bedrooms. One even has three for larger groups." He pushed open a door and gestured for her to enter.

The room still held a full-sized bed with a brass frame, a tall bureau, and a nightstand—all covered in a thick layer of dust. The window looked out over the front of the cottage, revealing a lovely partial view of the bay.

Tia's eyes blurred with tears as she turned to face them. "I love it. Thank you." She pivoted slowly, taking in her new home. "It's awfully big though. Maybe one of the smaller cottages would be better for me?" Although she'd always admired this particular house, she didn't need two bedrooms. Maybe it would be better to save it for future guests.

From the doorway, Meg cleared her throat. "Um, how would you feel about having a roommate?"

Tia looked up sharply. Living by herself was lonelier than she'd expected, but she wasn't keen on the idea of moving in with a stranger. On the other hand, it was a two-bedroom house. If sharing the space was what it took to live in this cottage, she'd seriously consider it. "A roommate?"

"Yeah." Meg met her gaze. "I think it's about time I moved out of the apartment over my parents' garage. What do you think about sharing the cottage with me?" She quickly added, "I totally understand if you don't want to though. You're probably used to living on your own."

Tia shook her head. "No. I'd love to have a roommate." She grinned impishly. "But, I don't know. How do you feel about mint chocolate-chip ice cream? If you don't like it, that's a dealbreaker."

Meg laughed. "I love it. I wouldn't complain if we had a freezer full of ice cream."

Tia crossed the small room and held out her hand to Meg, who grasped it firmly. "Deal." They shook hands, then both dissolved into a fit of laughter. Meg appeared as giddy about the opportunity to live there as Tia was.

Shawn and Zoe had gone down to the first floor while Meg and Tia checked out the bedrooms.

"Meg?" Zoe shouted up the stairs. "Celia called and said there's someone waiting for you at the Inn."

Meg paused on the landing outside the bedrooms. "Who is it?"

"I don't know." Zoe's voice floated up to them. "But you'd better check it out."

Meg shrugged and Tia followed her down the stairs to go meet Zoe and Shawn outside.

"So, what do you think?" Shawn asked.

"I love it." After living in a series of small, rundown apartments, Tia could hardly believe she'd get to live on the resort property. She swallowed hard and swiped at her eyes. "Thank you both."

"No problem." Zoe beamed at her. "I'm so glad you like this idea." She turned to Meg. "You'd better get going. Celia said whoever it is didn't seem very patient."

"I'm going, I'm going," Meg grumbled. She took off at a brisk walk, covering ground quickly.

"Who's waiting for her?" Tia asked out of curiosity.

Zoe's eyes twinkled. "You'll see. We had surprises for both of you today."

Tia laughed. "Okay, then. I hope hers is as good as mine." Before heading back to the Inn, she took a final look at the cottage and her heart warmed. There was no way Meg's surprise could be anywhere near as wonderful as what they'd given her.

20

Meg

Meg strode purposefully away from the cottage, but slowed her pace as she rounded the bend. Whoever was waiting for her at the Inn could afford to wait a few extra minutes. It was too wonderful a day to hurry, and she wanted to savor what had just happened.

When she and Zoe had initially discussed fixing up Cottage Twenty for Tia, Meg hadn't intended to ask Tia to share the space. They'd chosen that particular cottage because Tia had mentioned to Zoe how much she loved it, not because of its size. After seeing the interior, though, Meg had been struck with a sudden desire to live there too. It made sense—Zoe, Shawn, and Celia already lived on the property. If Meg lived there, too, she'd be closer to work and readily available if something came up at the resort or one of the events.

Her brain was a mess of jumbled thoughts, but the stillness of the narrow gravel lane running in front of the cottages and the sound of the waves lapping at the sand below the cliff brought peace to her heart. Postponing her dream of renovating the barn hadn't been something she'd foreseen, but was for the best. They were only about a week and a half away from October and the barn wasn't anywhere near empty enough to begin renovations. At this rate, she'd be lucky to have it done by January or February.

Thinking about how much junk remained in the barn saddened her and she paused for a few seconds to gaze back toward the cottages. She was too happy about the prospect of living at the resort to allow her worries to ruin the day. Visions of morning jogs on the beach and evenings spent with friends and resort guests on the Inn's porch filled her head. And, although she'd lived on her own for a while, it would be nice to have a roommate again.

When the Inn came into sight, Meg noticed a tall figure standing on the porch. At first, she thought he was a guest, but as she drew closer, she realized it was Taylor. What was he doing at the Inn on a Saturday morning?

A few stray wisps of hair tickled her cheeks, and she swept them back up into her low ponytail before climbing the steps to the front porch.

"Did we have plans for today?" Meg asked Taylor.

He leaned against the railing and regarded her with a soft smile. "Nope. *We* didn't have plans."

She cocked her head to the side, feeling as confused as Tia had been an hour earlier. "Okay?" she said, drawing out the single word.

His grin spread. "Well, as you may know, I'm currently unemployed because there was a fire in the restaurant I manage."

She winced. She'd thought he'd forgiven her for the fire, but now she wasn't sure.

His eyes widened and his smile faded. "No, no. I'm sorry. I shouldn't have said that."

The screen door opened, and Celia stepped out, leaning on her silver walker. She carefully closed the door behind her, leaving her little dog Pebbles staring forlornly at them through the mesh. "I think what Taylor is trying to say is he's here to work on the barn with you."

Taylor nodded gratefully at Celia. "Yes." He turned to Meg. "Does that work with your schedule?"

Meg mentally ran through her day. The wedding that afternoon was so small that Zoe and Tia wouldn't need her help. Everything else she'd planned to do could be pushed to another day. If Taylor was offering to help her with the barn, she wasn't going to turn him down. Actually, it almost felt like the universe had heard her concerns on the way back from the cottage and was providing her with a solution.

She stepped closer to him, smiling so widely she could feel the corners of her eyes crinkling up. "I think I can make that work, and I'd love the help. Thank you." Once again, he was giving up his free time for her. He truly was a great friend. In all the time she'd dated Theo, he'd never supported her the way Taylor did. An odd sensation rippled through her chest and her breath caught.

Before she had time to dwell on what she was feeling, Taylor crossed in front of her, pausing at the top of the steps. "Are you ready to get started?"

Meg glanced at Celia, who hadn't moved away from the door. The elderly woman's lips had curved into a secretive smile. Nothing about this situation was overtly out of the ordinary, but something was up.

"Have fun, you two." Celia's eyes twinkled and she looked like she was having a difficult time keeping a straight face.

"Oh, I'm sure we will," Meg said. Even though the other days she'd spent clearing out the barn with Taylor had been hard work, they'd been surprisingly enjoyable.

Taylor tapped his fingers against the porch railing, looking over at her. "Meg? You coming?" He walked down to the grassy lawn below and paused again to wait for her.

"Yeah, sorry." Meg jogged down the stairs toward him. Behind her, the screen door closed softly as Celia went back inside. Meg looked down at her hands. "I should have grabbed our gloves."

"While I was waiting for you to get back from the cottages, I took the liberty of bringing the gloves and masks out to the barn. I knew you kept them in the mud room, and I figured you wouldn't mind."

She looked up at him, her heart warmed by his thoughtfulness. "Thank you."

He shrugged, but didn't make eye contact with her. "No problem."

Meg hesitated for a second. Why was he acting so oddly all of a sudden? It reminded her of how he'd reacted at the catering kitchen the month before—friendly one moment and awkward the next.

They passed through the thicket of trees behind the Inn and came out near the barn. Its wide doors were halfway open, creating a gaping dark hole in the exterior. A twinge of unease ran through Meg. There was still so much to do before they could even think of remodeling the structure.

She focused on the brightly hued flowers she'd planted around the foundation. Yes, getting the barn ready was going to take a lot of hard work, but it would be worth it. The air around them seemed to buzz—not with sound, but with a heady sense of anticipation.

"All right, let's get this party started," Taylor said loudly as they approached the entrance.

She narrowed her eyes at him.

When they stepped onto the concrete floor of the barn, a loud cheer erupted from every direction. "Surprise!"

Meg blinked several times until she could see in the dim light.

All of her family were there—her parents, Sam, and Libby with her husband and kids. The staff of the Willa Bay Lodge's kitchen huddled together, clutching brooms and leather gloves. Cassie, Kyle, and their children smiled at her as they climbed down from the loft.

"I thought you could use more help than just me," Taylor said matter-of-factly.

Meg's vision blurred and she whispered, "Did you put this all together? For me?"

He chuckled. "Yep. When I brought up the possibility of a work party, everyone was excited to help. We all know how much this place means to you."

She burst into tears, overwhelmed by his generosity and that of her other friends and family.

"Honey? Are you okay?" Her mom's voice rose over the murmur coming from the rest of the group. She started forward to comfort her daughter, but Meg's father reached out for her arm to hold her back.

Taylor put his hand on Meg's shoulder and asked quietly, "Do you need a minute?"

She nodded, pressing her lips together firmly to stem the flow of happy tears.

"I'm just going to take Meg outside for a minute to fill her in on the game plan. In the meantime, if you'd like to get started, grab a pair of gloves and a dust mask," Taylor announced. He gestured to a pile of equipment near the door that Meg hadn't noticed when they'd come in.

Libby stepped forward and clapped her hands. "Alright, you heard him. Let's go, people."

Galvanized by her sister's bossiness, everyone moved in unison toward the safety equipment while Taylor led Meg out of the building. He took her back into the privacy of the grove of trees near the barn, toward a bench nestled against a tall cedar. He made sure she was settled before sitting down next to her.

When she'd calmed sufficiently, she searched his face. "You organized all of this for me?"

He nodded, gazing at her softly.

"Why?" she asked. Her heart beat faster as he reached for her hands, covering them with his own. His fingers intertwined with hers, and she couldn't help but notice how muscular they were, and feel the roughness of the light calluses he'd earned from working in the kitchen. She'd seen them work magic as his knife flashed nimbly through a stack of vegetables, but now she was having trouble reconciling the attractive man in front of her with her friend and former boss.

He took a deep breath. "Because I'd do anything for you."

They locked eyes and she found herself lost in the passion she saw there. A thrill shot through her. Was this really happening? Did she want this?

He smiled at her and brushed her hair with one hand, then caressed her cheek with the other and leaned down to kiss her gently on the mouth. His lips touched hers for only a few seconds before he pulled away, scanning her face.

She wasn't sure what he saw in her expression, because she was frozen in place, her head buzzing with a myriad of emotions. Taylor had kissed her. Cassie had been right all along that he had feelings for her. And, as much as Meg had brushed off her friend's suspicion that the attraction was mutual, she couldn't deny it now. She definitely wanted this.

She stared at Taylor, her breath coming in shallow bursts. How had it taken her this long to realize how wonderful he was? He was her good friend, someone she'd always felt comfortable confiding in. They shared a passion for cooking and had spent countless hours together in the kitchen. Had this been simmering under the surface that whole time?

Taylor reached and tentatively stroked her cheek, breaking her out of her trance. While he was still smiling, his expression was tinged with fear. At that moment, she wanted nothing more than to assuage any doubts he had about her feelings for him.

She stretched up and circled her arms around his neck. He grinned, and snaked his arms around her waist, scooting her along the bench seat until their bodies were enticingly close. The stubble along the nape of his neck tickled the pads of her fingertips as she nudged his head down so she could plant a bold kiss directly on his lips. The woodsy, clean scent of his aftershave swirled around her. Kissing Theo had never felt like this.

Out of the corner of her eye, Meg caught sight of Zoe, Shawn, and Tia, who'd halted along the path about ten feet away from the bench. Shawn was feigning interest in a tall oak tree next to him, but Zoe and Tia didn't bother to hide the huge smirks on their faces as they looked on.

Meg broke the kiss and Taylor looked at her, startled. She jutted her chin out to indicate the presence behind him and he turned to look, his face reddening when he saw who'd arrived. He released her, but kept one arm around her waist.

Meg eyed Zoe. "You knew about all of this, didn't you?"

Zoe laughed, her eyes filled with mirth. "That I'd find you and Taylor kissing in the woods?"

Meg tilted her head to the side. "Ha-ha. I meant the work party."

Zoe giggled. "Yeah. I knew about that too." She and the others walked past the bench and she called over her shoulder, "Do you think the two of you will be able to find time today to help with the barn?"

Shawn elbowed her in the side and Zoe shot him a sassy look. Tia covered her mouth, but couldn't hide the laugh that burst free before she hurried off toward the barn. Zoe looked back at them again and winked, then grabbed Shawn's hand and followed Tia.

When they were out of sight, Taylor chuckled. "We'd better get back. Everyone is probably wondering where we are."

She raised her eyebrows. "Oh, I doubt they'll be wondering for long. I'm sure Zoe will have told the whole group about seeing us here." She shook her head ruefully. "My mom is going to be so happy. She never liked Theo much, and she loves you."

He stood, and offered her his hand. "Well, then. I guess we shouldn't disappoint your mom, or the rest of them." Meg took his hand and stood, and he pulled her close again, gazing into her eyes. "Is this what you want? Do you want a relationship with me? This is your last chance to change your mind before we head back to the barn."

She nodded vigorously, choking back tears. "Yes. This is what I want. I want you. I want us." Again, she was struck with joy and wonder that she hadn't seen it before. Ironically, it had taken her quitting her job and not seeing him as much to make both of them realize how much they cared for each other.

He twined the fingers of his right hand through her left and ran his thumb over her knuckles, sending shivers up her spine. They walked back to the barn, hand-in-hand.

While her family and friends pretended not to know about their new relationship, her mother looked happier than she had in months and Meg could tell Cassie was going to pounce on her as soon as they were alone. They all got to work, carrying junk out of the barn and sorting it into piles to keep, donate, or toss. By the time they'd broken for a simple lunch of sandwiches and fruit prepared by Celia, they'd made a noticeable dent in the contents of the barn. Zoe and Tia had to leave after eating to prepare for the afternoon wedding, but the others stayed until early evening.

After everyone else had left, it was just Taylor and Meg. They climbed up into the loft, and Taylor sat on the edge as he'd done the first time they were up there. Being near him gave Meg the confidence to sit closer to the edge, although she hadn't quite worked up the nerve to dangle her legs into open air like he did.

"I can't believe how much we got done," she said in awe as she took in the floor below. With over half of the stuff gone from the barn, it appeared more massive than ever. Her stomach fluttered. Although they weren't starting the remodeling for at least a few more months, it was really happening. Today had been a huge step toward her dream of owning her own restaurant.

"I know. And I think I've managed to talk everyone into coming back in another month or so if you and I haven't cleaned it all out by then." Taylor wrapped one arm around her waist and kissed the top of her head.

She leaned into him, loving the support he offered. Making this old barn into a fine dining establishment wasn't going to be easy, but she knew she'd get through it with him by her side.

21

Sam inserted her credit card into the gas pump and crossed her fingers that the transaction would go through. When it did, she breathed a sigh of relief. Although she'd been actively seeking a teaching job, nothing had panned out so far. Now that the school year had been in session for a few weeks, it was time to start looking for something else or her dwindling bank account would soon be as empty as her gas tank. She finished pumping gas and took her receipt, wincing at the total before getting back into the car.

She was running a little late for dinner at her parents' house, not because she had a valid reason, but because she was trying to prolong the inevitable. No one in her family knew that her teaching contract hadn't been renewed for the school year, and she wasn't looking forward to telling them. After how upset they'd been about her breakup with Brant, she'd hoped to find a new job before telling them she'd lost her former position.

Unfortunately, she was getting to the point where she'd have to move into the apartment over her parents' garage as soon as Meg vacated the premises.

As she was pulling up to the curb outside their house, her purse vibrated. She put the car in park and grabbed her phone quickly in an attempt to answer before the caller hung up.

"Hello?" she said.

"Hi," a man answered. "I'm trying to reach Samantha Briggs."

"This is she." She held her breath, hoping he was calling about a job at a local high school, although that seemed unlikely so many weeks after school had started.

"My name is Andrew Hodgins. I'm calling from Bayside Prep School." He cleared his throat. "We received your application a few weeks ago."

Her brain quickly ran through the applications she'd sent out. Bayside Prep wasn't ringing any bells. After seeing that there weren't any jobs at the other local high school, she'd cast a wide net and applied for so many positions that she couldn't remember them all. Where was this school anyway? She hoped it wasn't too far, because she really didn't want to move away from her family and friends.

"Ms. Briggs?" he asked. "Are you still there?"

"Yes, sorry." Even if she didn't remember applying to his school, a job was a job. "Thank you for calling me."

"Well, thank you for submitting an application for our Physical Education department." He hesitated. "You're probably wondering why I'm calling."

"I am, a little," she admitted. "School has been in session for a few weeks, so I wasn't expecting to hear back about any jobs at this point."

"Well, we weren't planning on hiring anyone else this

year either, but things have changed. Are you still interested in a position at Bayside Prep?"

She glanced at the front window of her parents' house. People moved around inside, readying everything for dinner. If she had to move away from Willa Bay, she'd miss these family get-togethers.

She took a deep, silent breath, then said, "I would love to hear about the job."

"I'm not sure how much you know about our school, but we're a small private school just north of Willa Bay and we have about three hundred students between grades six through twelve. About two-thirds of our students board with us and the rest come from the local communities."

A boarding school? She hadn't realized the area had any boarding schools. But, then again, she didn't have kids or had any reason in the past to look into jobs at such places. It sounded like something she'd like to know more about though.

"Interesting." She nodded, even though she knew he couldn't see her. "What is the position you're looking to fill?"

"It's for a middle-school PE teacher. Our current teacher had to leave suddenly for a pregnancy that became high-risk."

"Oh." Sam's good mood deflated. "So, you're looking for someone for a short-term absence."

"Yes, but it will probably last until the end of the school year." A door opened in the background and he said, "Can you hold on a moment please?"

"Sure." She glanced at her parents' house again. In all likelihood, she'd already been spotted, and they'd be wondering why she was still sitting in her car.

A minute later, he came back on the line. "Sorry about that. My assistant had an urgent question."

"No problem," she said automatically.

"So does this sound like something you'd be interested in? If so, we'd like to set up an interview for later this week."

She nodded vigorously. "I'm definitely interested."

"Great! How does Friday at one o'clock sound?"

"Let me check my schedule." She went quiet for a moment and looked at the calendar on her phone, even though she was fairly certain she didn't have anything planned for that date. She was free almost every day unless she was scheduled to work at her mom's catering company, but she didn't want it to seem like she was desperate for a job. "I'm free on Friday afternoon."

"Good. I'll have my assistant send you directions to the school and some other information."

They exchanged goodbyes and hung up. Sam logged the appointment on her calendar and then opened her car door. As soon as her feet hit the walkway, Libby's youngest daughter, Kaya, ran out of the house and flung herself at her aunt.

Sam wrapped her arms around Kaya. "Hey, sweetie."

"She's been waiting at the window for you to come in," Libby said from the doorway. Her hands were folded across her waist as she leaned against the doorframe, but she appeared less stressed than the last time Sam had seen her.

Samantha released the little girl and stood up, then reached for her hand. They walked into the house together and Kaya pulled her over to the corner of the living room where she'd placed a few stuffed animals against the wall. Picture books were scattered across the floor in front of them.

"Look, Auntie Sam! My stuffies are going to school!" Kaya beamed.

"I see that." Sam crouched down and picked up one of the books. "How do they like school?"

Kaya scrunched up her face. "Little Bunny was kind of scared, but I think she's getting over it now."

"Ah." Sam looked over at Libby, wondering why Kaya was suddenly so interested in school.

"Kaya's going to be starting preschool next week at the same school where the other kids all went," Libby said brightly. "Gabe is working full-time at a new job and I'm working more at the catering company, so we figured it was time for her to go to preschool." She turned so Kaya couldn't see her face and said in a quieter voice, "I'm going to miss her during the day though. I think I'm more upset about it than she is."

Sam gave her sister a quick hug. "I'm sure she's going to have a great time playing with other kids her age there."

"I know." Libby brightened. "And at least Gabe finally has a job. That's a big weight off of me."

"I'm glad you're feeling better." Sam smiled at her. "How's Mom doing?"

Libby cocked her head to the side. "You know, she's doing surprisingly well. She said she has something exciting to tell us tonight."

Sam raised her eyebrows. "Maybe Mom and Dad are finally going on that trip to Italy that Mom's talked about for years."

Libby shrugged. "I don't know, but whatever it is, she seems happy."

"Okay everyone, time for dinner," Debbie called out. "Kids, go wash your hands."

Libby's kids thundered off toward the bathrooms and

Sam wandered into the dining room, where Taylor and Meg were chatting with her parents and Gabe.

"Hey." Sam waved at everyone, then went into the kitchen. Debbie was in the process of removing a giant pan of lasagna from the oven. "Do you need any help, Mom?"

"If you could get the oven door, that would be great." Debbie carried the unwieldy tray into the dining room and set it on a long hotpad in the center of the table.

Sam shut the oven door and followed her Mom out to the table. The kids were just trickling back in, and she quickly found her assigned seat next to Meg. Her older sister was sitting close to Taylor, and Sam could tell they were holding hands under the table. Sam grinned, but didn't say anything. After her date with Taylor, she'd suspected he had a thing for Meg, and hadn't been a bit surprised when he'd suggested a work party at the barn.

Seated at the head of the table, her dad said a prayer as they clasped hands. When he was done and everyone had a plate full of food, Debbie clinked her fork against her water glass to catch everyone's attention.

Even the kids stilled as Debbie made her announcement. "I'm sure all of you have noticed that I've been a little out of sorts lately."

Tommy, Libby's youngest son, said, "Yeah, you've been a little grouchy." His mom hissed at him from across the table and his eyes grew wide. "Sorry, Grandma."

Debbie laughed. "Don't worry about it. I'm sure I haven't been easy to live with." Her eyes scanned over everyone. "Many of you know that my friend's death hit me hard. I'd like to do something to honor her, so I've decided to organize a fundraising event for a local cancer charity in Diana's memory."

"Oh wow," Libby's eyes sparkled. "Mom, that's awesome!"

"That's such a great idea," Meg said. "I'm sure all of us would love to help."

"Definitely," Sam said, watching her mother's face. Debbie's smile widened even further seeing the support of her family. Her enthusiasm was contagious, brightening Sam's own sagging spirit. With a possible new job on the horizon, things were turning around.

"Thank you, girls." Debbie beamed at them and Peter regarded his wife with pride. "Also, I've decided to hire an assistant to help out with the catering business to give me a little breathing room." She looked at Libby, as if seeking her approval. "Does that work for you?"

Libby nodded. "If that's what you need, I'm fully behind that decision."

"Let us know what we can do to help with the fundraiser, okay?" Sam took a bite of the lasagna, savoring the tangy sauce, gooey cheese, and perfectly spiced meat. There was a reason why her mom's catering business was so successful.

"I will." Debbie grinned, then looked around. "Does anyone else have any news to share?"

Sam set her fork down. "Well, I have a job interview on Friday."

Libby stopped eating. "A job interview? Do you not like working at the high school?"

Sam tried not to squirm and met her sister's stare head on. "The district had some funding issues and my contract wasn't renewed for this term."

"Oh no," Meg said softly. She patted Sam's arm. "These past few months have not been kind to you."

Sam sighed and looked down at her plate, then back

up at her family. "You know, maybe it's been for the best. I think my life needed a little bit of a shakeup."

"What is the interview for?" Debbie asked. Next to her, Peter continued to shovel food into his mouth.

"A private school in the area, Bayside Prep. Have you heard of it?" Sam said.

Debbie nodded. "It's supposed to be a great school."

"I've heard really good things about it," Libby said. "That's exciting. You'll have to let us know how it goes."

"I will." Sam breathed more easily than she had in weeks. She'd been concerned that her family would be upset about her not telling them she'd lost her job, but they were taking it better than she'd expected.

"We have some good news too." Libby smiled at her husband. "Gabe's been offered a full-time position with the company he's been temping for."

"Oh, honey, that's wonderful." Debbie sighed with happiness. "I'm so thankful that everything seems to be working out for all of you girls, even if it's been in a roundabout way. We're so glad to have Taylor with us today." She shot a meaningful look at Meg, who immediately blushed.

Taylor grinned. "I'm happy to be here." He gazed lovingly at Meg.

"Yeah. I'm glad you're here too," Sam said. "It takes some of the attention off of me. What took you so long to ask Meg out anyway?" She wiggled her eyebrows at him.

Taylor's face turned as red as Meg's. "Uh..."

Sam laughed. "I'm just kidding. But seriously, I'm glad you're here." She meant it too. She'd never seen Meg so relaxed and happy as she was tonight with Taylor. It gave Sam hope that, one day, she would meet someone who would make her light up as much as Meg did around Taylor.

~

Meg

That Friday, Meg and Taylor picked up BBQ pork sandwiches in town and brought them back to the Inn at Willa Bay to eat. They spread a thick, plaid picnic blanket on the ground outside of the barn and laid out the feast. Although they'd only officially been dating for a week, their longstanding friendship made it seem like they'd been together forever.

They leaned against the exterior wall of the barn and ate their sandwiches while watching the sun sink below the horizon. This time, she didn't mind when he wiped a smear of BBQ sauce away from her face, and he didn't panic and run away after doing so. Taylor wiped his hands off on a paper napkin and tucked their garbage away in the sack their food had come in.

"I think we should be able to get most of it done after the cleaning party next week," he said. "Then there should just be a few odds and ends left that you and I can take care of."

"Do you think so?" Meg craned her head back to look up at the broken window in the loft. They'd barely touched everything stored in the upper floor of the barn last time.

He nodded. "You'll see. It'll all get done. Don't worry." He wrapped his arm around her shoulders and pulled her close.

She snuggled into him, grateful for all he'd done for her. Without his brilliant idea to host a work party, there was no way they'd be anywhere near done with the task of getting it ready for renovations. She carefully wiped off her fingers to ensure she'd removed any trace of BBQ sauce and stretched forward to pluck the journal out of her shoulder bag.

She ran her fingertips over the leather cover. She'd almost finished it, but still hadn't come any closer to knowing what had happened to Davina. Had she left Willa Bay to seek a life elsewhere? Would they ever know?

Whatever the case may be, the young woman's journal had brought many good things into Meg's life. When she'd been worrying about the barn not being ready, the recipes had gained her a regular feature on Coffee Talk Seattle, a basis for the menu whenever she did open her restaurant, and a connection to Taylor as they cooked for the grand opening.

She set the book on her lap and rested her head against Taylor's arm. Although she didn't have her restaurant yet, the barn itself had been a big part of her life for the last few months, more so than she could have ever predicted. She and Taylor may have spent over a year working together in the Lodge's kitchen, but the time they'd spent alone in the barn had given them the opportunity to finally get to know each other.

The sun had completely disappeared from sight, and the blue sky had evolved into a mesmerizing patchwork of pinks, oranges, and purples. The temperature had dropped along with the sun and she shivered as she put the journal away. When she sat back down next to Taylor, she huddled close to him to share his warmth. She tipped her head up, searching his face in the waning light.

He smiled softly and kissed her on the lips before stroking her hair back away from her cheeks. "Thank you for sharing with me your dream for the barn."

She smiled back at him. "Thank you for believing in it just as much as I do. I don't think many other people could see my vision for it." She winced at the memory of Theo seeing the barn for the first time, then looked back at Taylor. The kindness and love she saw in his face erased any thoughts she had about Theo.

"It's important to you, so it's important to me," he replied.

"Thank you." She wrapped her arms around his neck and kissed him again, then let her arms fall to his waist, snuggling close to enjoy his warmth again. The outer wall of the barn was rough against her back, but that didn't bother her. The old structure had its flaws and had seen its own share of history, but it also held her dreams for the future. It truly was her haven by the bay.

EPILOGUE

Tia

Tia yanked on the roots of a waist-high thistle stalk, leaning back with all of her body weight, but it refused to budge. She tugged again, and suddenly, the weed pulled free and she fell backward, cradling a handful of thorny green stalks against her body like it was a small child. She lay back on the ground, laughing at the absurdity of the situation.

Native plants had long ago overtaken Cottage Twenty's gardens, but she'd discovered that some of the heartier, original inhabitants of the garden had survived, including a gnarled yellow rose bush in the backyard. While Shawn had his construction crew working on the interior of the house, she, Meg, Zoe, and Cassie were trying to whip the yard into shape. Libby and Sam had been helping too, but had left about an hour ago to get dinner started in the Inn's kitchen.

She cast the uprooted weed aside and rested her arms on the ground, her hair splayed out against a patch of grass as she gazed upward. A few puffy clouds dotted the blue sky, and if it weren't for the cool breeze that ruffled her hair every so often, she wouldn't have believed it was already the end of September. The summer season was coming to an end and the autumn leaves would soon be falling. She couldn't complain though. It had been a better summer than she could have ever imagined—a new job, new friends, and now a new place to live.

"Are you okay?" Cassie loomed above her like a giant. Her blond curls gleamed in a ray of sunlight that snuck through the curtain of trees surrounding the cottage.

Tia laughed again and sat up, the blood rushing from her brain with the sudden movement. "I'm fine." She pointed to the long thistle. "I finally won the war."

Cassie eyed the remaining weeds lining the foundation of the building. "Uh, I think you may have won a battle, but there's still some fighting left to do."

Tia looked in the same direction and frowned, but even the thought of how much they had left to do couldn't dampen her spirits. Shawn had promised her and Meg that his crew would have the cottage ready to move in by the end of October, and she intended to have the yard cleaned up by then. Cassie and the others had graciously volunteered to help with the cleanup, and they'd turned it into an impromptu midweek get-together of their Wedding Crashers group.

"Maybe," Tia said brightly and grabbed her small garden trowel. "But I'll show them who's boss." She stood and waved the pointed end of the tool at the weeds menacingly.

Cassie backed away, her eyes dancing merrily. "I'll leave you to it. Libby called and said dinner will be ready in a few minutes." She glanced at her watch. "I should check in with Kyle to make sure everything's okay at the bakery."

"He's worked there before though, right?" Tia asked.

Cassie shrugged. "Yeah, but never for a full day on his own." Her eyes darted to her watch again before she took a deep breath. "You're right—I'm sure he's fine. And the kids are used to going there directly after school now."

Tia grinned and shook her head. "Just give him a call. That way you won't spoil your dinner with worrying about him and the kids."

Cassie bit her lip as she weighed her options, then sighed. "Okay, okay. I'm trying to get better about trusting Kyle and giving up a little control over everything, but it can't hurt to just check in." A soft smile spread across her face. "Things are going so well with him that I don't want to mess anything up."

"I'm sure he won't mind," Tia said firmly. She didn't know Cassie well, and wasn't sure what had caused her divorce, but she'd seen how much happier Cassie was now that she and Kyle had rekindled their relationship. Any man that was willing to take a vacation day from work to manage his wife's bakery so she could be with her friends was a man worth keeping.

Cassie pulled her phone out of her pocket. "Thanks, Tia. I'm going to give him a call." She tapped on the phone a few times, then said to Tia, "Remember, it's almost dinner time."

"Yes, Mom," Tia teased.

Cassie walked away while holding the phone to her ear, and Tia picked up half of the pile of weeds she'd accumulated to deposit them in the wheelbarrow near the front porch. As she came around the corner of the house, Zoe was propping up her rake against the siding. Meg came around from the other side and removed her leather work gloves. "I'm so ready for dinner."

Zoe chuckled as she examined the palms of her hands. "Me too. And I'm ready to take a break for today. My skin is getting torn up from all of this gardening, even with the gloves."

Tia checked her own hands for calluses. "Mine too." She surveyed the front yard. Zoe and Libby had made a ton of progress, mowing the scrubby grass and weeding the front flower beds. Judging by the pile of tree limbs in the corner of the yard, someone had been trimming branches as well.

"Are you ready to head out?" Cassie asked. She'd been pacing the graveled lane in front of the cottage while talking to Kyle. If the goofy grin on her face was any indication, all was well at the bakery—and in her relationship with her ex-husband.

"Yep," Meg said. "Taylor's going to join us for dinner too. He wanted to help out today, but he had some things to take care of at the Lodge." Her face lit up as she said her boyfriend's name, and Tia's stomach twisted with envy.

Meg deserved all the happiness in the world and Tia didn't begrudge her finding it with Taylor, but when was it going to be her turn? *Stop it, Tia*, she chided herself. Her life had already changed so much in the last year. She needed time to adjust to her new surroundings and circumstances. At the moment, there was no room for romance in her life.

The others started to walk toward the Inn. Zoe stopped and looked back at her. "Are you coming?"

Tia shook her head. She wanted a couple minutes alone to let everything soak in. "I'm going to finish up with what I was doing. I'll be right along." She gave them a little wave, and they continued walking.

She watched the three women talking and laughing together, until they'd disappeared around the bend in the road. She returned to the backyard, gathered up the rest of the weeds she'd extracted, and dumped them in the wheelbarrow. Instead of leaving immediately for dinner, she sat on the top step of the front porch and let her gaze drift.

Slivers of blue peeked through the trees and she could hear the water lapping softly against the shore below. The air was scented by the freshly cut grass and churned damp soil below the porch. The breeze she'd felt earlier intensified and she wrapped her nylon jacket tighter against her chest, but she didn't want to leave yet. This was like her own secret garden, tucked away from the rest of the world.

Like the other times she'd been to this cottage, she was overtaken by a strong sense of peace and wellbeing. She'd never felt this way back home in Texas, where she was always under the watchful eyes of her parents and siblings. She frowned, thinking about how they'd reacted when she'd relayed the good news about her and Meg moving into the cottage.

Her mother had scoffed at the idea and warned against it. She insisted that Tia living in the same place as she worked could backfire and Tia could lose both her job and her home at once. As much as she tried to ignore them, her mother's words had formed tiny seeds of doubt in her mind. Was she doing the right thing by moving onto the resort property?

At the periphery of her vision, a robin chirped as it fluttered from one branch in a tree to another. Grateful for the distraction, Tia pushed herself off of the porch step. She stood in the middle of the lawn and turned in slow circles, her head turned up to feel the last rays of sun on her face. The tension eased out of her neck and shoulders as she breathed in the salty air.

Recent memories flooded into her thoughts—how capable and confident she felt while solving problems during events, Zoe's kindness in letting Tia share her small space, and the excitement on Meg's face when she proposed sharing the cottage with Tia. The truth was, Tia's family wasn't in Willa Bay, and they couldn't see how happy Tia was to work at the Inn and the friendships she'd developed there.

No matter what her parents thought, Tia needed the freedom to live her own life. Things wouldn't always be perfect, but she'd figure them out as she went along, just like she always had. One day, maybe her family would recognize her strength, but until then, she wasn't going to let their negativity ruin all of the happiness she'd found in her new hometown.

Author's Note

Thank you for reading A Haven on the Bay! If you're able to, please consider leaving a review for it.

Wondering what's in store for Tia? Find out what happens next with Book 4, The Sunset Cottages.

If you haven't read Willa Bay's sister series, the Candle Beach Novels, check out Book 1, Sweet Beginnings.

Happy reading!

Nicole

ACKNOWLEDGMENTS

Thank you to everyone who's helped me with this book, including:

Editor: Devon Steele

Cover Design: Elizabeth Mackey Design

Made in the USA
Las Vegas, NV
16 January 2021

16035605R00142